Sarah turned

And her heart ... whiteness of his face. She felt certain he had lost too much blood to live. She wished there was a real doctor nearby. She had never stitched up anyone who had been torn up this badly, and the thought of him dying as she worked on him suddenly upset her, making her feel shaken and alone. It was not the first time since she had arrived that she wondered if perhaps she had taken on more than one woman could manage.

She took a deep breath and braced herself while she washed her hands in the bowl of steaming hot water Kumani had prepared for her. "Lord," she prayed as she worked, "please save this man's life. Let him live. And, Lord, send someone out here to help me, please. I am afraid that I can't do all this on my own. I need Your help, Lord."

SALLY KRUEGER has seen much of the world. She was born in England and lived in Kenya as a child. She wrote her first published novel, *The Promise of Rain,* while living in Scotland for a short time. Sally is a school librarian and lives with her husband and four children in Alberta, Canada.

Books by Sally Krueger

HEARTSONG PRESENTS
HP256—The Promise of Rain
HP348—Some Trust in Horses

With Healing in His Wings

Sally Krueger

Heartsong Presents

A note from the author:
I love to hear from my readers! You may correspond with me by writing:

> Sally Krueger
> **Author Relations**
> **PO Box 719**
> **Uhrichsville, OH 44683**

ISBN 1-58660-609-3

WITH HEALING IN HIS WINGS

All Scripture quotations are taken from the Holy Bible, King James Version.

All of the characters and events in this book are fictitious. Any resemblance to actual persons, living or dead, or to actual events is purely coincidental.

Cover design by Gary Maria.

PRINTED IN THE U.S.A.

one

Sarah Cameron stood out in the hot Kenyan sun, staring in utter frustration at the group of tired Africans lounging in the shade of the huge old thorn tree. Red dust blew up around her face, then ran down her temples in rivulets of perspiration. She was standing in an open, flat space where the bush had already been cleared, but there was so much more to do—and at this rate it would take forever to clear the ground for her medical clinic. She would never get used to the fact that in Africa people did not work during the middle of the day.

Back at home in Aberdeen, Scotland, hiring someone to work for a day meant a full day's work. Yet, here on the equator, a Northern European work schedule was as foreign as frostbite. She tried to remember that in this part of the country, in the year 1922, the African people had had only one or two generations of contact with Europeans at the most. She must not expect them to work as if they were Europeans.

"Memsahib! Memsahib! Come quick!"

Sarah turned. Her houseboy, Kumani, was running down the path from her cottage, kicking dust up behind him and shouting and waving at her.

"Come at once, Memsahib! A man, a *bwana*, he is hurt, maybe dead already. Come quickly!"

She looked past Kumani and saw a crowd of Africans standing on the veranda of her little house, clustered

5

around someone they had placed on her examining table. Sarah began to run. All her medical supplies were up at the house. Until she could get a real building, she held her clinic on her wide, shady veranda.

"Who is it, Kumani?" she asked, as she caught up to him.

"I don't know. A hunter, I think. They are saying he must be dead. I just ran to get you."

The red dust of the road blew up into her face, covering her arms and legs. Her rumpled hat blew off, and she quickly stopped and picked it up, slapping it back over her short brown hair. Someone on the veranda caught sight of her coming.

"Memsahib, Memsahib!" The cry went up. "There has been a bad accident. The bwana has been gored by a rhino. He is dying."

As she ran, questions flew through her mind. Who was this man? What was he doing out here? Was he on safari? The nearest white people, as far as she knew, were Rev. MacDougal and his wife in Gilgil.

She bounded up the steps of the veranda, the Africans making way for her, and saw a blond young man lying on her examining table. His face was worse than white; it was utterly colorless. And there was blood all over his clothes, including what looked like a blood-soaked sheet wrapped around his stomach and another around his thigh. He must have already lost a tremendous amount of blood.

Quickly and carefully, Sarah pulled away the clothing from the wound on his stomach. A collective gasp went up from the crowd around her as the gash opened up and spurted more blood. Sarah quickly covered it again.

She would have to sew it up.

"Disinfectant! Kumani, get the disinfectant quickly. And the opium. Here is the key to my medicine chest. Now! Run!"

She wondered if any organs had been damaged. If they had, then the man would die. There was nothing she could do about that. Even if by chance the wound had missed his major organs, he may have lost too much blood to survive anyway, or more likely he would succumb to infection. It would be a miracle if he lived through this. But she would do everything she could for him. Including praying.

Kumani came running with the things she had asked for, and she went to work. First she gave the man an injection of opium; then she began to clean out the wound.

Sarah's mind was so concentrated on her job that she didn't hear the arrival of another group of people. But they were not in the urgent hurry of the group who had brought her the patient. In fact, they were a somber, quiet lot who laid their burden down gently on the grass in front of her home. Only when she had finished cleaning out the wound and was getting ready to sew it up did they make their business known.

"M'sabu?" A young man stepped up onto the veranda wearing a traditional Muslim caftan. "I have brought the other bwana. But he is dead." He nodded and glanced over his shoulder. Sarah followed his gaze and saw the body on the lawn, wrapped in a canvas tarp.

"Who are these men, and where do they come from?" she asked the young man.

"They are from Nairobi, M'sabu. This man is Jock Davis." He nodded at the lawn again. "He was on safari with that bwana, Peter Stewart." Now he nodded toward the patient. "A rhino charged Bwana Davis. Bwana Stewart tried to kill it, but he missed and it killed the bwana. And then it charged Bwana Stewart. He shot it again and wounded it, but it gored him too."

Sarah's mind raced. She had no idea what the procedure was in this country for dealing with accidental death like this. The MacDougals would know what to do. She would just have to send the body to them. She told the man, "You must take Bwana Davis to Bwana MacDougal in Gilgil. Tell him about the accident, and he will know what must be done. What is your name?"

"Juma."

"Juma, please explain to Bwana MacDougal that Peter Stewart is still alive at the mission station out here. Tell Bwana MacDougal that we must get him to the hospital in Nairobi as soon as we can, or he will die too."

Sarah went inside and emerged with a note and some money, which she gave to Juma. He and the others who had brought the body picked it up and set off down the dusty rutted track that was the road to Gilgil. It was early afternoon, and even going at walking pace, they could be there before dark.

Sarah turned back to her patient on the veranda, and her heart sank as she noted again the unnatural whiteness of his face. She felt certain he had lost too much blood to live. She wished there was a real doctor nearby. She had never stitched up anyone who had been torn up this badly, and the thought of him dying as she worked on him suddenly upset her, making her feel shaken and alone. It was not the first time since she had arrived that she wondered if perhaps she had taken on more than one woman could manage.

She took a deep breath and braced herself while she washed her hands in the bowl of steaming hot water Kumani had prepared for her. "Lord," she prayed as she worked, "please save this man's life. Let him live. And, Lord, send someone out here to help me, please. I am afraid that I can't do this on my own. I need Your help, Lord."

Two hours later, as the afternoon sun started dropping behind the big thorn trees to the west of the house, Peter Stewart was still alive and Sarah was still sewing, with careful, painstaking stitches. Much later, when Kumani was lighting the hurricane lamp on the table behind her, she tied off her last thread and reached for the disinfectant and the bandages. She, Kumani, and Kamau, the cook, lifted the patient gently and carried him into her bedroom, where they laid him down on her bed. She pulled the mosquito netting around him and tucked it under the mattress.

Sarah was exhausted. At least Peter Stewart still lived, though she wondered for how much longer. She sent Kumani off to the kitchen to fetch her some supper and went out into the fresh night air. Kneeling down beside a big, soft chair, she prayed for the life of the stranger on her bed. After she had eaten her supper, she set up a cot beside her own bed where the young man lay, and she lay down to sleep there. Briefly, before dropping into an exhausted sleep, she wondered if he would be alive when she set eyes on him in the morning sun.

But Sarah woke up before dawn. She lay on the narrow cot, confused about where she was. For a minute she thought she was still in the narrow bunk on board the ship traveling around the Horn of Africa. Then, in the pale pearly predawn light, she saw the mosquito netting of her own bed rising up in a pyramid beside her, with the body lying inside, and she remembered. Her heart sank.

"Please, Lord Jesus, let this man be alive," she whispered as she lifted the netting. "Please preserve his life and heal his terrible wounds. You are the only doctor I have, and I am depending on Your healing power to give him his life, Lord Jesus. And if he doesn't know You, then I pray that through this experience he will come to know You and give his life to You."

She reached over and touched his neck. When she felt the very faint beat of his pulse, she let out a long sigh of relief. She hadn't even realized she had been holding her breath. Since it was still too dark to see anything much, Sarah lay back down and tried unsuccessfully to sleep.

When the sun finally appeared over the horizon and sent its first long rays through her window, she got out of bed again and studied the man's face. There was the faintest trace of color in it this morning, a very good sign. She put the netting down and tucked it in again. The man didn't stir, and his eyes remained closed. She wondered if they would open again, ever.

Knowing there was nothing more she could do now, she gathered her clothes and got dressed in the closet. When she emerged from her room, Kumani was just knocking on her door with the morning tea tray. She saw a *toto,* a small African child, standing behind him.

"M'saab," he said, "Bwana MacDougal sent a toto from Gilgil to say that he has contacted the doctor in Nairobi, but there is a big typhoid epidemic there, and he cannot come to help you. He also says that the funeral of

Jock Davis will be tomorrow."

"Thank you, Kumani," Sarah said, taking her tea from him. She knew the MacDougals slightly. They were young American missionaries who served Gilgil and the surrounding district. Ethel MacDougal had mentioned several times that they should have tea and get to know each other a little better. Sarah had agreed, but she didn't know when she would have time to travel all the way to Gilgil just to have tea and visit. There was so much work to do here, and being the hardworking Scotswoman she was, she always felt slightly guilty when she was not actually working.

Most Sundays, she traveled to Gilgil in the old lorry she had been given by the missionary society to attend the service at the MacDougals' church, but she rarely stayed to visit anyone afterward. Although the MacDougals often invited her to stay for lunch at the parsonage, she felt it would be rude to accept their invitations too often. Besides, one of the reasons she was able to live out here in the bush by herself was that she was used to her own company. And if the truth be told, she had to admit she was afraid of social situations. In fact, she had suffered all her life from a debilitating case of shyness. At last she had found something to do with her life where she didn't have to deal with other people in social situations at all. Surely it was a gift from God.

She smiled to herself as she remembered the day she knew for certain that God was calling her into the mission field. She had already been taking her nurse's training when the great missionary and Olympic athlete, Eric Liddell, had come to speak at her church in Aberdeen. She had been utterly overwhelmed by Mr. Liddell's passion to give his life in service to others and thrilled to the core when he spoke of the need for strong Christian men and women who could endure hardships and loneliness to go out into the mission field and spread the gospel to the millions who had never heard it before. And now, here she was a missionary and a nurse in the wilds of East Africa. Of course, she had applied to go to China like Mr. Liddell, but she was informed that East Africa was a place where medical missionaries were in great demand, and they had assigned her to this little spot of wilderness three hours' drive from Nairobi. And once she got her clinic up and running, she would start giving Bible lessons to the children and doing Bible studies with the adults too. She could hardly wait. If only she could get the Africans to work faster!

She turned to look at her patient again, wishing she had a doctor here to consult with. The fact that she had been able to sew the man up and that he had not died during the night was a miracle in itself. But his injuries, and the subsequent infection which would surely set in soon, were far beyond her nurse's training.

Sarah poured herself some more tea, and as she sat by the bed sipping thoughtfully, she noted that he breathed evenly, but shallowly. She wondered if he had broken some of his ribs. She had tried to feel them last night but wasn't able to tell. If he had broken a rib, even if it was possible to take him to Nairobi, it might be dangerous to move him over the rough track, studded with potholes and boulders, in the back of her old lorry. It could cause his rib to puncture a lung.

The morning sun was now shining like a spotlight right through the netting onto his face. Sarah stood up and lifted the netting, tying it in a knot above the bed. As she leaned over the bed, she must have bumped it a little bit. There was a groan. Looking down she found herself staring into a pair of strikingly blue eyes. She grabbed the glass of water from the bedside table and dipped a clean flannel cloth into it, which she gently pressed to the man's lips. The eyes closed again. She pressed some more water onto his lips and put her hand on his forehead to feel for a fever. He was hot. She took another cloth, wet it and laid it over his eyes, then turned and closed the bedroom curtains. Well, the decision was made: She would not take him to Nairobi if he was running a fever. But she must send a message to Dr. Mainwaring at the hospital, asking for the medicine her patient would need and any advice he might be able to offer her. She would also ask him to send her a doctor as soon as one could be spared.

Sarah decided not to go to Jock Davis's funeral, as she did not want to leave her patient. She sent a message with a toto for Rev. MacDougal to contact the hospital by radio and get the message to Dr. Mainwaring to send her help as soon as possible.

As the morning passed, Peter's fever grew fiercer and hotter. Sarah spent all day with him, trying to keep it in check, bathing his body with cold water, changing the dressings on his wounds, and giving him the medicines the doctor had sent from Nairobi. Now and then she took a walk out to see her new clinic's progress, which was about as slow as her patient's.

Sarah slept on the cot beside the bed in her own room again that night. It was uncomfortable, and she woke up every few hours to cool Peter off. Three days later, Sarah was utterly exhausted. But the man still lived.

One morning when Kumani brought in Sarah's tea, he stopped for a minute at the door to her room before leaving.

"What is it, Kumani?" Sarah asked, knowing this was Kumani's way of letting her know he wanted to tell her something.

"I have heard a rumor that it was the fault of Bwana Davis's gun bearer, Juma, that the rhino charged the hunters. Some of the men are saying that he had tried to shoot a snake in the path and spooked the rhino. They say that the *Askaris*—the police—have been to Gilgil to question him, but they cannot find him." Kumani paused as if trying to decide whether to tell her more.

Sarah waited. She was slowly learning to be patient, knowing that if Kumani decided not to tell her, she wouldn't get a word out of him no matter how much she pleaded or demanded. But in a minute Kumani spoke. "I have heard people say that Abdul, Bwana Davis's man, started this rumor because he dislikes Juma. They say he and Juma fought during the entire safari. Abdul thought Juma was incompetent. Anyway, Juma has disappeared, so perhaps this is not a rumor and he really is guilty."

Sarah wondered what would happen next. Would there be some sort of inquiry into Jock Davis's death, or would it just be considered an unfortunate hunting accident? She hadn't been in Africa long enough yet to know how far the law of England reached into this remote corner of the Empire.

That afternoon Sarah decided to take another quick walk over to check on the excruciatingly slow progress of the ground clearing for the clinic. As she was walking down the red path, she heard the whine of an engine in the distance. She rapidly turned and ran back up to the house. At last, someone was coming to help her. She prayed it was an actual doctor, or at least someone with some more medical supplies and antibiotics. She arrived at the bottom of her veranda steps just in time to see a motorcycle with a sidecar pull up. A woman climbed out of the sidecar and removed a pair of goggles and a large scarf. At first Sarah didn't recognize her, but when the woman turned to face her, Sarah stopped in amazement. Ethel MacDougal! Rev. MacDougal's wife was roaring around the countryside on a motorbike.

"Well, hi there, Sarah!" Ethel's friendly American welcomes always caught Sarah off guard. She was more used to the politely reserved greetings of her Scottish heritage.

"Good afternoon, Mrs. MacDougal. What a surprise to see you here."

"Ethel! Please, call me Ethel, for goodness' sake. Here we are in the wilds of Africa; surely we can at least be on a first-name basis! I heard you were nursing a very sick patient, and I thought you might just like a bit of company, so I persuaded Ralph to give me his new motorbike and a driver and let me come up for a visit."

Ethel laughed. Then noticing Sarah's look of amazement as the driver of the motorcycle started it up again to park it over in the shade of a tree behind the house, she added, "Do you like my motorbike? Actually, Ralph uses it to travel around the district. It's so much cheaper to run than a car."

"Yes, I suppose it is," Sarah replied, staring at it.

"So, tell me about the poor man you're looking after.

We just had Jock Davis's funeral, you know. The poor widow came all the way from Nairobi, and she seemed terribly upset. Although, between you and me, I don't think she'll be spending her entire life as a widow. She's no Queen Victoria, if you get my drift!" Ethel walked up the steps to the veranda. Sarah followed dutifully behind, as if it were Ethel's home, not hers.

Ethel was a small, pretty woman who was a bundle of energy and enthusiasm. She was never at a loss for conversation, and most of the time when she wasn't talking, she was laughing. She was the perfect wife for her rather serious husband.

Ethel plunked herself down on one of the chairs that Sarah kept to the side, away from the examining table and chairs she used for her patients during her clinic hours. "My goodness, it's hot. You don't happen to have a cool glass of lemonade or iced tea handy, do you?"

Sarah called Kumani and asked him to bring them out something.

Ethel, fanning herself with her scarf, continued. "I understand there's going to be a bit of an inquiry into the whole accident. Have you heard anything about that yet? But no, that's another subject. Tell me, my dear, how is your patient doing?"

"He's still got a fever, and I'm treating him for an infection, but it's really too soon to tell if he will recover. But I am praying for him. I only wish there was a doctor who could help me. I am really quite out of my depth with his injuries."

"Ralph and I are also praying for him. And for you too, my dear. You are an awfully brave woman to be living out here alone like this. I do admire you so. And now you have this man to deal with as well! I spoke to Mrs. Davis, the widow, at her husband's funeral yesterday. She tells me Peter Stewart has no family here in Kenya. He's Scottish, so he is one of your countrymen. Other than that, she says she doesn't know much about him. He hasn't been in Nairobi very long, and apparently, this was the very first safari he went on as a guide. Dreadful luck, isn't it?"

Sarah nodded.

Kumani brought a jug of orange juice and some glasses. Ethel drank hers gratefully.

"I don't suppose the poor man is a Christian, is he?"

"I don't know," Sarah replied. "He hasn't recovered consciousness."

"Well, that is something else we must pray for. If he recovers, he'll need to hear the gospel. We must just pray that God doesn't take him until he has had a chance to accept Jesus as his Savior and Lord! Now, tell me, Sarah, how are you managing? You do look tired."

Sarah smiled weakly. "Yes, I am tired. I don't sleep very well because I am always listening in case Peter, I mean, Mr. Stewart's fever gets worse or he becomes delirious."

"You poor thing. Up here all alone and caring for a man on the brink of death. You really must take a break for an afternoon and come and have tea with me. You'll wear yourself out if you don't look after yourself too, my dear, and then you won't be much help to your patient either."

Sarah smiled gratefully. It was kind of Ethel to be so concerned about her, but she knew her first duty was to her patient. "I hate to leave him with Kumani while he is so ill, Ethel."

"Oh, Sarah, you're so dedicated to your work. I really do admire you, and I hope we can be friends. I'll tell you what. As soon as you feel you can leave your patient, why don't you send me a message, and I'll send the motorbike up to fetch you?"

"Thank you, Ethel. It is very kind of you to think of me like this."

Ethel stood up and started tying her scarf around her head. "Nonsense. I'm only being selfish. I need a friend as much as you do. We women must stick together, especially in the back of beyond here where we both find ourselves! Meanwhile, I'll be praying for you and for Peter Stewart's recovery. God wants us to have friends so we can pray for them too, you know."

As Sarah waved to the red cloud of dust that was Ethel's motorbike roaring off down the road, she had to admit that Ethel was right: She did need a friend, someone close by who could pray for her. Already she felt lighter and more cheerful just knowing that someone cared about her predicament and was praying for her and for Peter, as well.

Meanwhile, she still had her work cut out for her keeping Peter Stewart alive. Morning, noon, and evening she kept vigil beside his bed, anxiously looking into his face for a clue about when his fever would break. He was hot and red with the fever still. His body was wasting away, but he still clung to life. At night and in the mornings she prayed for him. As she prayed, she wondered, did he know and love God? Had he given his life to Jesus? Was he ready to meet his Maker, forgiven and free? Perhaps it was because Peter was not a Christian that God seemed to be very slowly, almost imperceptibly, healing him and giving him a second chance at life.

One afternoon Sarah received a note from District Commissioner Garth Oswald, the local colonial supervisor in Nairobi, telling her that he had sent a telegram to Peter Stewart's family in Scotland and had just received a reply. His parents said that their health prevented them from making a trip to Africa to see their son. Mr. Oswald asked her to care for him until the typhoid epidemic in Nairobi abated. He also mentioned that he would be in the area one day next week and would stop in to ask her what she knew of the accident, as he was conducting an investigation into it.

As Sarah cared for Peter Stewart, she began to wonder who he actually was. Day after day she studied his feverish face. She had seen him open his eyes only a few times, in his moments of delirium. They were as blue as the African sky after the rain, and they looked huge and unnatural in his gaunt face. Sarah's tired mind wandered through strange paths as she watched over him. Was he the younger son of a Scottish laird, who had done some evil deed and was sent off to Africa to start a new life? Or perhaps he was merely a poor sheep farmer who came to Africa to seek his fortune. Maybe he was simply the son of a shopkeeper who longed for a life of more adventure than taking over his father's business when he grew up. But still the fever raged through his body, and still Sarah kept a vigil by his bed.

Then one morning a large black touring car drove up Sarah's rutted road, leaving a huge red cloud of dust hanging in the air behind it. Sarah had been holding her clinic on the veranda as usual, and she and everyone there stood quietly, watching the vehicle approach. A large mustached man stepped briskly out of the side door, which his chauffeur held open.

"Good morning, Miss Cameron!" he said, striding up her veranda steps two at a time. "My name is Garth Oswald. I am the district commissioner from Nairobi. I hear you have a man here who was gored by a rhino. I've come to ask you what you know about the situation."

Sarah shook his hand. He looked around at the people waiting on the veranda and said, "May we go inside?" Without waiting for her answer, he strode over to the front door and held it open for her. Meekly, she went into the cool darkness, feeling as if he were about to question her about some unknown crime she had committed. Kumani followed them in, and she asked him to bring them tea and scones.

Mr. Oswald sat down at her dining-room table and took out a notebook and a pencil. "Well, Miss Cameron, I realize you weren't a witness to the accident, but we are trying to determine what exactly happened and if there was anyone at fault. Would you mind telling me everything you know about what happened?"

Sarah repeated all that had happened, and then told him what Kumani had told her.

"Yes, I've heard that story too," he said. "But with Peter out of commission and Jock dead, all we have to go on are the Africans' stories, and they have their own reasons for saying what they say. I doubt we'll get to the bottom of this unless Peter recovers and tells us what he knows." Mr. Oswald drained the tea from his cup.

"Would you like to see Mr. Stewart?" Sarah asked.

"No, I'll just take your word that he's pretty torn up. I only hope you're able to bring him through it, but with all the doctors busy with the typhoid epidemic, it'll be a miracle."

"Well, nothing is impossible for God," Sarah commented dryly.

"I suppose not, but I've yet to be convinced," he said, setting his teacup in the saucer and pushing his chair back. "Well, I'd better get back to town before it gets too late." He put out his hand for Sarah to shake. "Thank you for your help, Miss Cameron."

"I'm afraid I didn't tell you anything you didn't already know."

Mr. Oswald didn't deny it. He simply said, "Well, it was important to check everyone's story. Good luck with your patient, Miss Cameron. Keep me informed of his condition, would you?" Then he strode out the door, down the steps, and got into his car. His driver had started it already, and they disappeared in a cloud of red dust. Sarah and her patients stood watching as it got smaller and fainter, beetling across the dry plain toward the escarpment in the distance.

Sarah turned, and suddenly there was a burst of excited chatter from all the waiting patients. She realized that the district commissioner had come all this way for less than an hour of talk with her. Unnecessary talk too, most likely. Well, it was really no affair of hers. She had work to do.

That night Peter Stewart's fever broke. Sarah was sleeping, but she awoke as usual, just before dawn. The room was very dark and cold, and it was silent. She couldn't hear Peter's ragged breathing any more. He must be dead!

She sat up quickly. With shaking hands she fumbled

for her matches to light the candle. In those few seconds, she realized that she'd come to care for this unknown man who slept in her bed. Would she never meet the person behind those blue eyes? Would she never hear his voice? Would she even have the chance to tell him about Jesus? Or did he already know Him? She suddenly felt desperate. He must live!

The light of the candle flamed over the bed. Sarah lifted the netting and saw her patient's chest rising and falling in long, slow breaths. His face was paler, and there were no beads of sweat glistening on it. She put her hand on his forehead. "Oh, Lord, thank you!" He was alive. The fever had broken at last.

The eyes flashed open at the sound of her voice. "Who are you?" came the hoarse whisper.

two

"My name is Sarah Cameron," she replied simply. "Go back to sleep now."

"What happened?"

"You were gored by a rhino, but you'll recover." *I hope.*

He closed his eyes, and Sarah began to tuck the mosquito netting back in.

"Jock? Is he okay?" His eyes were open again, trying to find her.

"Don't worry about Jock. You need to sleep so you can get better." She spoke firmly but gently. He didn't have the strength to argue. He closed his eyes and slept.

Sarah closed her eyes too. As she lay listening to the even breathing of the man beside her, she suddenly felt uncomfortable sleeping here in the same room with a strange man. Now that she had actually spoken to him, he had become a person, not merely a patient. She quietly rose and picked up her blanket. She slipped into the lounge and sat down on her softest chair, pulling the blanket up and over her. She immediately fell into a deep sleep.

When she woke in the morning, she had a crick in her neck and her back ached. Kumani was just crossing the room with her tea tray. He didn't notice her curled in the chair. When she said good morning, she startled him so much he nearly dropped the tray.

As she sipped the tea, rubbing her neck in an effort to

get the kink out, she wondered if she should try to get hold of someone who could drive Peter Stewart to Nairobi in a more comfortable vehicle than her old lorry, now that he was over the worst. It was strange that no one had sent a message to ask how he was doing, but then hunters were often away for months at a time, so perhaps no one had realized that anything had happened to him yet. On the other hand, Jock Davis's death was public news, and in a small place like Nairobi, Peter Stewart's accident would not be a secret.

Sarah finished her tea and realized that she had left her dressing gown hanging behind the door in her bedroom. No matter, her patient would be sleeping. She got up and quietly opened the door to the bedroom.

"Who are you? Where am I?"

She jumped and turned to the bed. She reached for her old blue dressing gown and wrapped it around herself quickly. "I am Sarah Cameron," she said in her brisk nurse's voice. "How are you feeling this morning, Pet. . . um, Mr. Stewart?"

"I've felt better." He tried to lift his head up, but instead, let out a groan of pain. He lay back on the pillow.

"Don't move, Mr. Stewart. You're very lucky to be alive. You were gored by a rhino, and you have more stitches in you than my grandmother's best quilt." Sarah spoke in her professional tone, but she couldn't help smiling as she looked into Peter Stewart's eyes at last. It had been a long wait. She called for Kumani to bring a fresh glass of water for the patient. "You need to keep your fluids up, Mr. Stewart," she said.

"Am I back at home?" he asked, closing his eyes. "You sound Scottish. Is this Aberdeen?"

"Ach, no, you're still in darkest Africa, laddie!" She put on her thickest brogue. "But I'm from Aberdeen m'self, just aff t'boat." She paused. What was she thinking? She was joking with a man she had never spoken to in her entire life! But he was trying to smile at her gratefully, through his cracked, dry lips.

Kumani brought the water just then, and Sarah hastily recovered her professional demeanor and held Peter's head up so he could drink a little. He sighed and sank back into the pillow, exhausted. He closed his eyes.

Sarah stood watching him for a moment. She gathered some clothes from the cupboard and went to dress. Her heart was light and happy. Her patient would surely survive. But what on earth had possessed her to tease him like that? It must be the strain of the past days that had caused her to lose her usual shyness momentarily. She sat down and prayed as she waited for breakfast.

For the next week, Peter slept most of the time, waking occasionally to drink some broth or water. Sarah felt she could leave him alone now, and she went out more often to supervise the work on her clinic. Not much had been accomplished without her there to keep the workers motivated, but at least the ground was now cleared of trees. At last, the foundation could be laid. Sarah could hardly wait to have a place to receive her patients properly. The sooner she established her station, the sooner she would be able to request an assistant. Perhaps one day she could persuade the mission society to send a doctor too.

Sarah was ambitious. She wanted to make an impact on the disease and the suffering of the people around here. She knew that if she could just teach the people better methods of hygiene and give them proper medical care, they would be free from their fear of illness and disease. It was this fear that enslaved the people to superstition and witch doctors. Sarah could hardly wait to get her clinic going, but everything in Africa took so long to get accomplished. There were no decent roads, and the Africans were not accustomed to working through the heat of the day. But since they were not far from the equator, the heat lasted most of the day. Even the mail took a long time to reach her, while supplies and medicines took even longer. All in all, Africa was a tremendous lesson in patience, for which Sarah prayed daily. But like everything else in Africa, patience was a long time coming too.

At the end of the week, she decided to take Ethel MacDougal up on her invitation to visit her. She wanted to tell her that Peter Stewart was recovering. She left Kumani in charge of the patient. Then she dressed in a khaki skirt and a white blouse, cranked up the lorry, and headed off toward Gilgil.

The MacDougals' parsonage was a rough stone building with a tin roof, set in a dusty dry garden. Ethel rushed out to greet her the moment she pulled into the driveway.

"Sarah, you did come! I was afraid you wouldn't find time. When you weren't at church on Sunday, I wondered if your patient had taken a turn for the worse. Now come on in and have something cool to drink. You must be exhausted, driving all this way by yourself. I must really learn to drive, but Ralph tells me that there is no need to learn when I can have a driver at my beck and call. Men! They like to think we women are so helpless, don't they? But just look at you. There's nothing you can't do."

Ethel guided Sarah inside the cool lounge while she kept up a happy chatter. After seating Sarah on an old brocade armchair, she took a seat on the couch nearby and rang a bell for tea.

"Now, my dear, tell me all about Peter Stewart. Mr. Oswald dropped by the other day after he'd been up to see you, and he said you were coping nicely. But I would rather hear it from you."

"Peter's come out of his fever now," Sarah announced, "and I think he is going to be alright."

"Well, praise the Lord, Sarah! You saved the poor man's life. If that isn't just the most romantic thing I have ever heard of, I don't know what is! Tell me, what is he like?"

"It's hard to say," Sarah replied, taking a dainty little cake that Ethel passed her. "But he actually comes from Aberdeen, the same place I'm from! It is a small world, isn't it?"

"Sure is. So what did he say?"

"Very little, actually. He still sleeps a lot. He did ask about Jock Davis, though, but I simply told him not to worry about Jock. He hasn't mentioned him again."

"Well, what are you going to do with him now that he's getting better? I suppose you had better send him to Nairobi."

"Yes, but Mr. Oswald asked me to keep him here because of the typhoid epidemic in Nairobi. But he does want to interview Peter about the accident when he's well enough."

"Ah, so you are on a first-name basis with your gentleman friend, are you?" Ethel's eyes were twinkling mischievously.

"No, I'm not," Sarah protested. "I just got tired of referring to a man who was sleeping in my own bed as Mr. Stewart, that's all."

"In your own bed! But of course, I had forgotten about that. You wouldn't have anywhere else to keep him, would you? It's so romantic, though. You must admit that, Sarah Cameron."

"No, I don't admit anything of the sort, Ethel. The man is at death's door. That is not at all romantic. In fact, it's exhausting if you're the one trying to keep him alive."

But Ethel was not to be deterred. "That's what makes it so romantic, you silly thing! You've saved his life. Tell me more about him. Was he surprised to find himself in your care when he woke up? Tell me all about it! I'm just an old married woman, and I need a little romance in my dull life!"

Sarah laughed in spite of herself. She had to admit that it was nice to have a friend like Ethel, who teased her and cared for her and actually enjoyed her company. But if Ethel thought being married was unromantic, she should try being alone!

Men had never taken much of an interest in Sarah because, for one thing, she was so tall. She was almost five feet nine inches. She felt awkward and ugly. All the young men she knew at home in Aberdeen seemed to prefer the dainty, petite girls. But fortunately, she was just as clever as any boy in her class, and if she wasn't the kind of girl they would marry, she was at least clever enough to get a good education so she could go out and earn her own living in the world. It had been fairly easy for her just to ignore the male sex altogether, unless of course they needed her help as a nurse. And it had been a good strategy, she felt. Though sometimes, sitting alone on her veranda as evening fell, she had to admit it was lonely.

After she had told Ethel all she knew about Peter, Sarah spent a happy afternoon hearing all about how Ethel and Ralph MacDougal fell in love, married, and moved to East Africa. By the time she found herself cranking up her lorry, it was almost time for supper. Ethel had tried to persuade her to stay and eat with them, but Sarah insisted that she wanted to be back before dark. She hadn't been away from her patient for so long before, and she was beginning to worry in case he had taken a bad turn while she wasn't there.

Peter Stewart was awake when Sarah returned home just after dark. Kumani was sitting beside him, helping him drink a little water. He was even offering him some soup. Sarah smiled. She should have known Kumani would have been looking after Peter perfectly well. Nevertheless, she was surprised to feel a twinge of jealousy that the two men were having a pleasant conversation, Peter's first since he had arrived, and it did not include her.

"Well, well, you look as if you are on the mend, Mr. Stewart. Sitting up and everything!"

He smiled, and Sarah was surprised to see his eyes travel over her as if he was looking at her for the first time. When his eyes did meet hers, warmth and interest sparkled brightly in them. Sarah suddenly felt shy again. She couldn't think of anything else to say.

"Miss Cameron, Kumani tells me I owe you my very life. Thank you. I don't know what I'll ever be able to do to repay you!"

Sarah felt even more flustered. "Please don't mention it, Mr. Stewart. I was just doing what I have been trained to do. It was nothing. I'm only glad you were brought here in time. If not for the quick thinking of the men who were with you, it would have been too late. Now, how long have you been sitting up? You mustn't tire yourself, you know." She said all this very fast, and there was a brief silence when she had finished.

"Well, yes, I am feeling rather tired," Peter said. "I suppose you're right and I should lie back down." Kumani eased him down onto the bed.

Sarah could see that the movement was very painful for her patient, but she was gratified to see how gently Kumani handled him. She should really train him to help her. Perhaps when her clinic was finished, she could do that.

ôa

Two evenings later, Sarah walked back from the building site, hot and thirsty. The sun dipped quickly down to the horizon. She wondered if she would ever get used to the speed of the sunsets in Africa. She hurried up the pathway, quickly lifting her eyes to the east to check for clouds. It was really too soon to expect the rains, but everyone in Africa looked for them out of habit. Sarah felt that just being in Africa had made her more aware of the sky and the weather and the fragility of life.

She arrived at her veranda and strode up the steps two at a time. "Good evening!" said a voice.

Sarah jumped, gasping. She hadn't noticed anyone arriving by the road. But there, deep in her biggest rattan chair, was a reclining figure.

"My word, you gave me such a fright!" she replied.

She came closer. "Mr. Stewart! What are you doing out of bed? You are far too ill to move yet!"

"Nonsense. I don't know how long I've been lying there, but I know when I've had enough of staring at the ceiling. I got Kumani to move me out here. He wasn't too happy about doing it, mind you. And please, call me Peter. No one calls me Mr. Stewart. I'm liable to ignore you if you do." He smiled wanly. The long speech had tired him out, and he lay his head back against the chair.

"Well, the sun has set, and it'll be getting cool now. Why don't I help you back to bed?" she suggested gently.

"No! No, thank you, I mean. I'm tired of staring at white walls. I'm staying out here."

Sarah sighed. Well, now she knew one more thing about this Peter Stewart. He was definitely stubborn. She could tell Ethel that news. She could also see he wouldn't make a docile patient. But if he was well enough to watch the sunset, then he was well enough to discuss his future.

"I'm going inside to wash up for dinner. Would you like me to bring you anything to eat, Mister. . .I mean, Peter?"

"I'm game to try a little something. This liquid diet is getting rather dull, I must say." He leaned his head back again and closed his eyes. She had the feeling she had just been dismissed.

She told Kumani to bring supper out onto the veranda and to bring an extra plate for Mr. Stewart. Then she went to her office to change from her hot, dusty trousers and blouse into a cool dress. She wondered if Peter remembered their brief chat about Aberdeen. Probably not. It was just as well. It was time to send the man back to his life in Nairobi. No doubt he would have to be in the hospital for a few more weeks, but his own friends could look after him there. She had work to do here, and she didn't really have the time to be looking after such a stubborn man.

But once again, a funny feeling flashed through her. She would miss him when he left. She had actually grown quite attached to him.

Kumani had arrived with the dinner tray and was just lighting the hurricane lamp when Sarah came out onto the veranda, wearing a simple white cotton frock. It flattered her tall, slim figure, and the small lavender-flowered print on the neck and waist complemented the lighter, sun-bleached streaks in her dark brown hair.

"You look nice tonight," said Peter.

"Thank you," Sarah said briskly, sitting down in the chair next to Peter.

She felt self-conscious. Here she was having supper with a handsome young man, alone and far out in the wilds of Africa. She had spent so many hours looking into his face, hoping he would open his eyes, wondering what his voice sounded like; but she had forgotten that when all those things happened, he would look into her face, gaze into her eyes, and listen to her voice. She was finding it very unsettling.

"You know, I am rather tired," he said. "Perhaps you could just spoon some of the mashed potatoes onto my plate. I can only move one of my arms, anyway. I'll just have a couple of bites, and then I should go back to my bed, Miss. . ."

"Miss Cameron," Sarah said firmly; then she looked at his now-familiar blue eyes and added, "but please call me Sarah." She reached for the potatoes and put some onto his plate.

"Peter, perhaps we should discuss how we are going to get you back to Nairobi. Now that you are well enough to sit up, you had better get to a proper hospital and have a doctor examine you."

Peter took a forkful of potato and shakily brought the fork up to his mouth. He slowly and carefully chewed it and painfully swallowed.

"I'm sorry, but I'm getting rather light-headed. Could you help me back to bed, please, Sarah? Could we talk about it tomorrow?"

Sarah wondered if he was deliberately avoiding the subject, but got up and went around to one side of his chair. Kumani went to the other side. Gently they lifted the man out of the chair. Sarah was surprised at how tall he was, even though he was very thin and not terribly heavy. However, he winced with pain, and she could see that the gashes on his chest must be hurting him terribly as they lifted him onto his feet. His face had gone very white, but he was determined to try to walk back to bed. Sarah was relieved when she and Kumani were able to lay him down at last.

She still felt strangely shy, but she thought she should at least lift up the white cotton shirt she had given him to wear to check that none of his wounds had opened with all this movement. Gently, she lifted up the shirt and probed around his abdomen. His eyes were closed. "I'm sorry if this hurts you," she whispered. "I just need to make sure we didn't damage anything when we moved you."

Everything seemed to be fine. Sarah pulled his shirt

back down and looked at him just as he opened his eyes. Their eyes met. Sarah looked away first. She bustled about tucking in his bedclothes and his mosquito netting. When she dared to look at him again, his eyes were closed, and he seemed to be asleep. She tiptoed out of the room, closing his door quietly behind her.

She went out onto the veranda, where her supper was waiting. It was a little cold now, and she ate quickly, her mind agitated. She kept going over and over everything that he had said this evening. He was obviously used to having his own way; she could see that. She didn't appreciate the way he had overruled her orders to Kumani that he stay in bed. She had not seen any signs that he was a Christian either. But perhaps it was too soon for her to know that for certain. Still, she wished he had at least given her a small sign of his faith.

She leaned back for a moment and watched the last glimmer of light disappear in the western sky. The scented breeze that came through the bougainvillea at the side of the veranda was cooling fast. Perhaps she had allowed herself to daydream a little too much. After all, she was nursing a handsome man back to health, caring for him every day, and praying for his recovery. Perhaps it was only natural that she would fall a little bit for him. She hadn't done it consciously, but now that she thought about it, she had hoped he might be a Christian for reasons besides his own salvation. But she certainly would never allow herself, even in a daydream, to fall in love with a man who didn't love God.

Not that she had fallen in love with Peter, of course, but she did have to admit that she had grown subconsciously attached to him in the last couple of weeks, especially during the long, lonely nights when he was so terribly sick. That must be the cause of all these strange feelings that had thrown her off balance this evening. She had been daydreaming a little too much. Well, it was time to put an end to that.

She had another busy day ahead of her tomorrow, and she needed her strength. And she had things to do tonight before she went to bed. She had letters to write to her church family in Scotland, explaining her work and how the building of her clinic was coming along. She also had to get her diary up-to-date. She had gotten so behind with her diary lately, what with having Peter to look after each evening.

Yes, he must go back to Nairobi. . .as soon as possible. She would get him to give her the address of someone who could send a car down to pick him up. Surely he must have friends somewhere who would do that for him. She had done all she could for the man, and now he had to go.

Sarah finished her dinner and went inside. She worked on her correspondence and her diary, and she went to bed in the little cot in her study. But it was a long time before she fell asleep.

Her thoughts wandered to the man in her bedroom. She kept seeing the look in his eyes when she had walked onto the veranda after she had changed her clothes. What did the look in his eyes mean? Did he find her attractive?

Her heart gave a little skip, and she turned around onto her other side. This was ridiculous. Even if he did think she looked nice, it did not matter. She must go to sleep. She closed her eyes. But her thoughts started to wander once more. She saw him looking at her again. She caught the skip in her heart and turned over again. Would she ever fall asleep? The sooner this man left, the better.

three

Peter was very tired the next morning. He was paying a price in pain for getting out of bed the night before. Sarah asked Kumani to take the morning tea into his room with instructions to give him breakfast and look in on him throughout the morning. She dressed, had breakfast on the veranda, and set out to supervise the work on her clinic. She was tired and irritable from her restless sleep of the night before. When she remembered her thoughts about Mr. Stewart (she determined to refer to him formally no matter what he said), she was completely disgusted with herself. What on earth had become of her? It was time to make her thoughts captive to Christ again and focus on the task at hand. And she had much to do. She needed to supervise laying out the plans for the foundations. Perhaps there would even be time to start digging them.

Sarah came striding home at lunchtime with a purposeful bent. She would eat quickly and lie down for an hour. She hesitated for a moment as she came in sight of the veranda. Had Mr. Stewart decided to come out and surprise her again? She looked carefully, but the only sign of life was the bougainvillea petals trembling in the slight breeze. A slight pang of disappointment flashed into her consciousness. It annoyed her. No matter. She would soon get her thoughts back on track.

She went straight into the kitchen where Kumani was

preparing a tray of lunch. "That's alright, Kumani, I'll just eat here in the kitchen. I'm tired, and I want to go and lie down afterward. How is Mr. Stewart this morning?"

"He's in some pain because of the walking he did yesterday, but he ate some breakfast. I think he is sleeping."

"Good. If he wakes up, offer him some lunch." Sarah ate her own lunch of cold meat and bread. Then she went and lay down in her study. She heard Kumani go into Mr. Stewart's room and the sound of the two men's voices. But, thankfully, she fell fast asleep.

A little over an hour later she got up quietly. The house had a cool, empty midday feeling to it. The rooms were silent and shady, sheltered from the heat of the day by the veranda that surrounded the house on three sides. It was one of Sarah's favorite times of the day. She often sat in her study and did her accounts or wrote letters, enjoying the peace and quiet. But today she went right out onto the veranda. There was no sign of Mr. Stewart anywhere. Relieved, she left the house quietly.

Sarah walked slowly back up the path in the late afternoon sunshine. She must speak to Mr. Stewart about his return to Nairobi, and she must check his dressings as well. She decided she would bring up the subject while she was changing them. That way he wouldn't be able to escape. But as she approached the house, she saw him sitting in the big chair under her bougainvillea. An involuntary thrill of anticipation fluttered through her. Quickly she suppressed the feeling and put on a businesslike expression.

"Good afternoon, Mr. Stewart," she said firmly, as she arrived. "I see you are out enjoying the sunset again. I hope you're feeling no ill effects from your little escapade yesterday." She sat in a chair a little distance away from him.

"Good afternoon to you too, Sarah. I thought we agreed yesterday that we would be on a first-name basis, considering the rather intimate circumstances in which we both find ourselves." His eyes twinkled mischievously. "Please call me Peter."

Sarah felt the color rising in her cheeks, but she held her voice firmly in control. "Yes, we did agree, Mr. Stewart, but I reconsidered the matter, and I feel that it would be more appropriate to maintain proper decorum in our relationship. I am, after all, a missionary nurse from the Church of Scotland, and I should really observe the appropriate social conventions."

Peter Stewart smiled at her warmly. "Well, my mother always says that it is a woman's prerogative to change her mind, Miss Cameron."

Sarah was surprised and relieved. She had expected him to be much less agreeable. She smiled back and prepared to discuss the next issue. "Mr. Stewart, we really need to discuss your return to Nairobi. Now that you are well enough to walk, I feel you must make the journey to the hospital so that you can receive proper medical attention. Do you have anyone we can contact in Nairobi who could send a car down to fetch you?"

"Yes, I am sure I can think of someone. I'll just give it some thought, first. But Sarah—I mean, Miss Cameron—I have some questions. Do you mind if I ask you them first? Kumani tells me that Jock Davis is dead." His voice faded. "Is that really true? I can't seem to believe it. Did you see him before he died? I just can't believe all this really happened." He sounded almost as if he were about to cry.

Sarah suddenly realized that what she had known for almost three weeks now was brand-new to him. "I'm sorry, Mr. Stewart, it is true. Mr. Davis was killed by the rhino. He was dead before the Africans got him here. I told them to take him to Gilgil, where his family came to fetch him. They had his funeral in Gilgil over two weeks ago."

Peter didn't say anything. He stared at the setting sun. Sarah waited.

His voice was low and sad when he spoke again. "Did you see Juma, my gun bearer? Do you know where he is? I need to speak to him."

"Juma has disappeared. Apparently there was a rumor that he accidentally discharged one of the guns while you were stalking the rhino, and that's what caused him to charge you. He was the one who brought you here. I sent him to Gilgil to get word to Nairobi of your accident, but I never saw him again. Kumani says he has heard rumors that he is afraid he will be charged with murdering Mr. Davis, and so he has disappeared. No one knows where he went."

Peter sighed deeply, then clutched his ribs in pain. There was another long silence. This time Sarah broke it. "The district commissioner came here after the accident, but you were so ill then. He wanted me to notify him if, I mean when, you recovered. He wants to take a statement from you. You'll need to go to Nairobi as soon as possible to do that, as well as to receive proper medical attention, of course."

She paused to let that sink in. Then she added brightly, "I would take you to Nairobi myself, but my lorry has very poor springs and regularly breaks down. I'm afraid it would get you to Nairobi in worse condition than you left here."

Peter said nothing. Sarah waited. *Well, he does have a lot to deal with. I will change and wash for dinner while he decides what he wants to do.*

She left Peter by himself until Kumani arrived with supper. She had changed out of her trousers and into her white dress with the lavender flowers. Peter looked up when she came through the door. She gave him a hard, bright smile and sat down briskly opposite him. Then she bent her head and said grace. Peter was caught off guard for a moment, but he quickly recovered and chimed in with an "amen" at the end.

They ate in silence. Sarah watched the sun settling deep into a wide pool of orange and pink color, then deeper into reds and purples. It touched the tops of the hills in the distance. Kumani would come to light the hurricane lamps any minute now. She glanced at Peter out of the corner of her eye. He was watching the sun as well. But he must have noticed her glance because he said, "I think I'll remember the African sunset for the rest of my life."

"I will too," she replied, but her voice was barely audible. He probably hadn't even heard her. They watched the sun sink into the hills while the sky above it flamed pink, faded to purple, then mauve, then gray, and finally went dark. Kumani came and lit the lamps. Still they sat in silence, listening to the cicadas and the distant laugh of a lone hyena. The stars spread outward from east to west, and the insects began to buzz and gather around the lamp.

The peace and the beauty of the deep, great African

night flooded Sarah's mind and heart, washing away every thought but that of the Being who could create such an evening. God Himself must have poured His very heart and soul into creating this night. It must have been on a night such as this that Jesus Himself was born.

She glanced at Peter. He was quietly watching her. Quickly she turned away in case she gave away the now-familiar flutter of joy that leaped into her heart every time she saw him watching her. But she could tell that the beauty of the night had deeply affected him too.

They sat awhile longer, and gradually Sarah realized that the very silence they were wrapped in was drawing her heart close to this quiet, handsome man, closer than any words ever could. And with this thought, a sliver of doubt slipped into her mind. She must not let herself feel close to Peter Stewart. If she let her guard down, she might even fall in love with him, and she must not do that. After all, he was not a Christian. Besides, he would leave as soon as he got well, and she would be left with a broken heart to mend. She must break this spell he was weaving over her at once.

"Mr. Stewart, I need to tell Mr. Oswald, the district commissioner, about your recovery." The hurricane light that glowed on the table seemed to become harsh and bright. The night outside drew away like a wave slipping off an empty beach. She cleared her throat. "I am going to send a toto down to Gilgil in the morning to get word to him that you have now recovered sufficiently to speak to him about the accident. You could also send word with the toto to someone who could come here in a car and take you to Nairobi. Or, if you prefer, we could have Mr. Oswald come and interview you here, and you could return to Nairobi in his car. What would you like to do?"

Peter sighed again. "I am so sorry to have been such an inconvenience to you, Miss Cameron. You have looked after me above and beyond what I deserve, keeping me here and nursing me and feeding me. I hope I haven't seemed to be ungrateful for all your goodness to me. One day I'll be able to repay you for all your kindness. Yes, I suppose I must get back to Nairobi, but I'll be absolutely honest with you. I don't know a soul in Nairobi. Except Jock Davis, and now I've managed to get him killed."

Sarah was taken aback by the bitterness in his tone. How should she reply?

"I came out to Africa after the war and decided to set myself up as a safari guide," he continued. "I stayed in a rented room when I was in town, but most of the time I was on safari with any guide who was available to teach me the ropes. But the one I know best is up north somewhere, so he's no use to me. This was only my second safari as a guide, and it looks as though it will also be my last."

He stopped for a moment. Sarah waited for him to continue. He took a breath and went on. "I haven't spent enough time in Nairobi to make friends. My only friend is Juma, and apparently no one knows where he is."

Sarah felt sorry for him, but she was determined to hold firmly to her position. "Well, Mr. Stewart, you'll have to stay in the hospital then. If you would like, I could come and visit you when I am in Nairobi, but I am sure you will be completely recovered in no time, and then you can get back to work."

"Yes, I hope so." He paused, deliberating for a moment

on something. "Miss Cameron, if you would be so kind as to let me rest here for a few more days, I would greatly appreciate it."

Sarah opened her mouth to object and explain that he needed a doctor's care, but instead she hesitated, and she heard herself saying, "I suppose that you could stay a day or two. But tomorrow I'll send word to the district commissioner that you are well enough to speak to him about the accident. I'll ask him if he would like to come here to interview you; then perhaps you can make the trip back to Nairobi with him. It'll be a day or two before he can make the trip out here, I'm sure."

Peter nodded as she spoke, but he didn't say anything. They sat together in silence for a few moments. Peter seemed glad, even relieved that he was to stay here a few days more. And she had to admit that she would be glad of his company. She must be getting used to him. It was surprising to sit so comfortably in silence with a man she hardly knew.

Peter was the one to break the silence. "Perhaps you would be so kind as to help me return to bed," he said softly.

Sarah stood up. "I'll get Kumani."

"No, don't. I want to try to walk with only one person helping me today. The sooner I recover, the better. If you could just come over here on my bad side and help me out of the chair, I think I can do it."

Sarah bent over next to his chair, and he put his arm around her shoulder. She eased him up, and together they went limping into the house. He was only slightly taller than she was, and when she turned to him, his face was close to hers. His eyes were filled with pain, but behind that she read a steely determination. Peter was silent, and his face was very pale. However, he was determined not to say anything to give his suffering away. Sarah helped him to her room and carefully lowered him until at last he lay on the bed, white-faced and gasping. She pulled the mosquito netting down. He lay with his eyes closed, his chest heaving. Her breath was coming fast, and her chest was heaving too, but for a very different reason.

"Good night, Mr. Stewart," she murmured.

"Good night, Miss Cameron." She could barely hear his whisper.

&

In the morning, Sarah sent word to Mr. Oswald that Peter was well enough to speak to him about his accident and that he needed a lift to the hospital in Nairobi. She prayed that Mr. Oswald would come quickly and take Peter away. After all, as a nurse, a missionary, and a Christian woman, it was really very improper to have a man staying in her home.

Besides, there was a more desperate reason to be anxious for Peter Stewart to go to Nairobi. The feel of Peter's arm around her shoulder and the weight of his body leaning on hers as she helped him into the house had stayed with her all night long. She had not been able to sleep until it was very late, as the memory of his body near and close to hers replayed in her senses over and over again. It was still with her when she had awoken this morning. Sarah felt ashamed and embarrassed with herself for having spent the night in the throes of these feelings. She wondered if she was falling in love. She had never been in love with anyone before. The sooner Peter Stewart left, the sooner she would be able to go back to her old, comfortable ways.

Friday morning was clinic day, one of the times when the Africans came to Sarah's house for medical treatment. Usually there was already a crowd of people waiting for her by the time she woke up, and this Friday was no different. There were children with runny noses, burns, or cuts. There was usually a pregnant woman or two, and sometimes there were men who had been fighting and had swollen eyes or cut lips. Sarah lined them up and examined them one by one, dispensing medicine and ointments as needed.

She was about halfway through attending to her patients when the door of her house opened and Kumani stepped outside, supporting Peter. He took him to the big chair and eased him down into it. Sarah found herself acutely aware that Peter was watching her, which made her lose her concentration. She dropped her stethoscope. She suddenly had trouble remembering her Swahili. And the more embarrassed she became, the worse it got. With a lot of difficulty, she managed to set her mind back on the child with the rash on his torso that she was examining. He had been here last week, and his rash did not look much better. Sarah tried a different ointment and squeezed a week's supply into a small bottle for his mother.

She moved on to the next patient. Each patient that she examined became an ordeal for her. She simply could not concentrate at all with Peter's gaze on her constantly. By the time she was finished seeing everyone, Kumani had already brought lunch out, and Peter was at the table waiting for her. She ran inside to wash up and slid into her chair, far more exhausted than she usually felt.

She said grace and added a quick silent prayer that Mr. Oswald would get her message and come to fetch Peter Stewart immediately. She turned to Peter and asked how he was feeling. He was a little sore, he said, but he felt he was getting better.

Peter's appetite was improving, and he was very adept now at eating with one hand. Sarah sliced his meat into smaller pieces for him, though. "I've sent for the district commissioner, and I'm waiting to hear when he will be able to come. I'm sure he'll be able to take you back to Nairobi in his car," she announced cheerily.

Peter cleared his throat. "Sar. . .Miss Cameron, I must speak to you about something." He paused. He seemed to be searching for the right words. "I'm afraid I had a rather bad night last night. I was not able to sleep very much because I was doing a lot of thinking. I just want to reiterate how deeply grateful I am for all you have done for me since my accident. I don't believe I would have recovered at all if not for the prompt and expert care you were able to give me. Please understand me when I say that I owe you my very life, and I am utterly indebted to you and always will be."

Sarah turned away. "Anyone would have done the same thing," she mumbled.

"It's because of your kindness toward me that I am reluctant to ask you for one more favor. You have already done so much. But the thing is, Miss Cameron, I had a rather bad war. I was hit by shrapnel. It nearly killed me, and the doctors tell me there are still a few pieces embedded in my skull. I had to spend many weeks in the hospital, first in a temporary army hospital up at the front. Then I had to be transported back behind the front lines as soon as I could be moved and was finally taken to London.

"My brother was also sent to the front. He was badly wounded, and he suffered for several weeks before he eventually died. They sent him to London, to the same hospital where I was. I was with him when he died." He stopped speaking, overcome with emotion. Sarah waited while he collected himself.

"Anyway, Miss Cameron, the upshot is this. I simply cannot go back to a hospital. I swore I would rather go back to the front than let myself be trapped in one of those places again, with all the suffering and the dying and the utter helplessness of anyone to do anything about it!" Peter's voice became harder and more bitter with every word he uttered, until finally he practically spit the last words out of his mouth like poison.

Sarah stared at him. "I. . .I'm so sorry," she whispered. "But you can't stay here either. It simply isn't proper."

"I know. I just need to think." He paused. "Of course, I realize I can't stay with you, but if you could just give me a day or two before sending me off to Nairobi, I think I would be well enough to look after myself. Then I wouldn't have to stay in the hospital at all. Sarah, I know it's a lot to ask of you after all you've done for me, but I would be eternally grateful if you could just keep me here for a few days longer."

Sarah felt a sudden rush of compassion. She had seen with her own eyes what the war had done to soldiers. She knew better than most how much they suffered. Another idea suddenly occurred to her. "If there really is no one in Nairobi who would be able to take you in and look after you, then perhaps I could arrange for you to stay at one of the missions. At the French mission, for example. The monks take people in all the time."

"Thank you. I suppose that would be the best plan." He looked at her and smiled. But it was a sad, lonely smile, and Sarah had to fight the urge to change her mind and tell him he could stay as long as he wanted with her. These very thoughts made his departure so important.

"I have sent word to Mr. Oswald. When he lets me know which day he's coming here, I'll make arrangements to have you taken to the French mission. I'm sure you'll be comfortable there. It is nothing like an actual hospital."

"Thanks. I appreciate it." Peter sounded defeated. Sarah felt terribly guilty, but she simply could not explain to him that the feelings she was developing for him were the reason he had to leave.

They finished their lunch in silence. Kumani took their plates away when Peter suddenly said, "My father was a doctor in Aberdeen, you know."

"Dr. Stewart? I did my nurse's training under a Dr. Stewart. You couldn't be Dr. Stewart's son, could you? He was the best doctor in Scotland!"

"Yes, that's my father, Dr. George Stewart of Aberdeen."

Sarah didn't hear the bitter tone in his voice. She simply couldn't believe her eyes. This man here on her veranda was actually Dr. Stewart's own son! Dr. Stewart was one of the kindest, wisest doctors Sarah had ever known. She had learned more from working with him than anyone else. He expected nurses to be medically well-trained and to use their training for the betterment of their patients. He didn't treat nurses like scullery maids either, as was the practice of many other doctors. Dr. Stewart had been an inspiration to her. "It couldn't be true," she found herself stammering. "Dr. Stewart is really your father?"

Peter nodded. "Yes. He suffered a stroke a few months ago, though. My brother's death has been very hard on him and Mother."

"Oh dear, I am so sorry to hear that. What a blessing that you weren't also killed when you were charged by that rhino. That would have been unbearable!"

"Well, it wouldn't have been such a terrible tragedy as my brother's death. Hugh was following in my father's footsteps. He was going to take his medical training as soon as he returned from the service. It would have been better for my father if I were the one who died and Hugh had lived."

Peter seemed to have forgotten she was there. He stared out into the blue, misty hills on the far side of the Great Rift valley. Then he began to talk, more to himself than her. "And now I have managed to get my client killed too. Only the second one I have ever had. My life is worse than a waste. It is a liability." He suddenly looked at Sarah and laughed, a twisted, bitter laugh.

"You can't be responsible for accidents, Peter. You can't be responsible for accidents or wars. People die in both of them, and no one can do anything about it." She spoke passionately, but he smiled at her as if he saw her from a great distance.

"Are we on a first-name basis again?"

Sarah felt he had trapped her, but she recovered quickly.

"Well, since I know your father, I suppose that makes it different."

"Thanks, Sarah." But there was no warmth, only irony in his voice.

Sarah suddenly felt she wanted to get away from this whole strange new complication in her life. She should go and see if the foundations of the clinic were finished, but it was too early. The workers would still be resting in the midday heat. And she had to admit she could use a rest herself after her morning's work. She lay back on her chair and closed her eyes. Peter must have been resting as well because neither of them heard the toto approaching. They both were startled when he spoke.

"Memsahib Cameron."

Sarah's eyes flew open. Standing in front of her was a small African boy, barefoot and dressed only in shorts, smiling broadly at the start he had given her. He held out a piece of paper.

"Oh, thank you, Kioko. Here's a sixpence." Sarah pulled the tiny coin from her pocket, and he bounded off down the path like one of the small indigenous dik-dik antelope. She unfolded the piece of paper and read it. Then she looked at Peter. He had closed his eyes again. "Peter?"

He opened his eyes. She looked quickly away. "Mr. Oswald says he is unable to come until Wednesday. He asks if you can wait until then, and he will take you up to Nairobi himself. He says some questions have arisen to do with the accident that he wants to discuss with you." She paused and looked at him. "I'll ask Ethel MacDougal if she could send word to the French mission that you'll be in Nairobi on Wednesday and you want to stay with them."

"Thank you, Sarah. I am sorry to continue to be such an inconvenience to you. But maybe I can alleviate some of the problem by moving out here onto the veranda. I'm really much better, so I don't need to be using your bedroom any longer. If you have a cot, we can just have it moved out here, and you can return to your own bed."

"But, Peter, your stitches are not properly healed yet, and you are still so weak. Besides, that cot is terribly narrow and hard. You can just stay in my room until Wednesday. It's only five days from now."

"Are you using the cot, Sarah?"

"Well, yes, but I'm healthy, and you're not!"

"I'm healthy enough. Besides, now that I know what you are sleeping on, I won't sleep a wink thinking of how uncomfortable you are because of me. No, Sarah, I insist. I am sleeping on the veranda tonight. I asked Kumani where my guns are, and he said that Juma left them here. I'll keep my rifle beside me and shoot anything that moves or slithers. I'll just be fine." He smiled warmly and confidently at her.

Sarah's heart gave a flutter of pleasure as she looked into the disarming grin on his face. She had been right about this man the first time he spoke to her. He certainly was good at getting what he wanted. She decided to surrender gracefully. "Fine, you can sleep on the veranda."

He smiled, too, and changed the subject. "I wonder what questions Mr. Oswald has encountered. It sounds rather ominous, doesn't it? I must go and visit Jock's wife as soon as I possibly can. I feel so awful about Jock. I can't stop thinking about the accident. I should never have come as close to the rhino as I did. I know full well how bad tempered and unpredictable they are. I should have been much, much more careful. But someone fired a shot. Kumani tells me they are saying Juma was the one who did it. Something isn't right. Juma was too experienced to fire a gun by accident." Peter was silent again.

"But accidents really do happen, even to the most experienced people," Sarah replied, realizing it was a rather feeble argument. Peter said nothing.

Sarah stood up. "Well, Peter, I must get back to work. I've got more patients to see. Please try to rest this afternoon and don't think too much about the accident. You'll need all your strength for the trip to Nairobi on Wednesday."

She had to admit she would miss him when he was gone. Even in the couple of days since he had become well enough to carry on a conversation, she had begun to feel that she had known him for a long time. Perhaps it was because she knew his father. But she was glad she had work to do. The feelings that had started to simmer in her heart when she thought of him made her nervous and even frightened. She thought back to the long night she had spent remembering the weight of his body as she helped him to bed, and her face burned with embarrassment. If he knew what she had been thinking, he would make her drive him to Nairobi this very instant! Thank the good Lord he couldn't see into her uncontrolled heart. Soon he would be gone, and her feelings would return to being normal and sensible. The sooner the better. On Sunday she'd go to church in Gilgil and speak to Rev. MacDougal about getting in touch with the French mission. After that, two more days of work, and then Mr. Oswald would come and take Peter away.

four

The next few days did not go exactly as Sarah had planned. For one thing, Peter got better faster than she thought he would. He was obviously a very determined man who intended to do everything in his power to recover. When she returned from the clinic Saturday afternoon, she found him pacing gingerly back and forth across the veranda, holding onto the back of one chair and moving on to the next. He was bent on getting "back under his own steam" as soon as it was humanly possible.

"Mr. Stewart, you'll just get sick again if you exhaust yourself like that!" Sarah scolded, as she rushed up the steps to guide him back to his chair.

"I am fine, Miss Cameron; you don't need to coddle me anymore." But he allowed her to put her arm around his waist and move him toward his chair.

"Yes, I do! Obviously, you are not sensible enough to give your wounds time to heal, so that leaves the job to me."

"I think I am perfectly capable of understanding how much stress my own body can take, thank you, Miss Cameron." His voice was cold and formal. She settled him into his chair.

"Mr. Stewart, I am a nurse, and I am the one who sewed you up. I know what your body can take and what it can't. It can't take all this movement so soon. If you're not careful, you'll tear out your stitches, and you'll be stuck here for another three weeks. Now sit still and don't move. I'm going in to change."

Sarah turned on her heels and strode off into the house. "Men," she muttered to herself as she put on a clean shirt and a pair of khaki trousers. "They never listen to anyone. The sooner Peter Stewart is off my hands the better! Thank goodness tomorrow is Sunday. I need to talk to Ethel and tell her how completely irritating this man is becoming!"

Sarah noticed that Peter had actually tired himself out rather badly, because as soon as Kumani had taken the supper plates inside, he asked her to help him back over to his bed in the corner of the veranda. They hadn't spoken much at all, but when she had helped him up out of his chair and taken his weight onto her shoulders, she was startled to hear him whisper, "I'm sorry, Sarah, you're right. I did do a little too much today."

She turned to face him and found herself looking right into his deep blue eyes. Ever so slowly, he leaned toward her. Her heart stopped beating, she forgot to breathe, and the next thing she knew, he was pressing his lips to her cheek. A rush of warmth flooded right through her and took her completely off guard. She almost dropped Peter onto his bed and fled into the house, calling over her shoulder, "I'll send Kumani out to help you with your pajamas."

❧

Thank goodness, thank goodness, it is Sunday, she thought as she awoke in the morning and the memory of the kiss came flooding back through her whole being. She would have lunch with Ralph and Ethel MacDougal after church, and she would not have to face seeing Peter until late this afternoon. She dressed in her lavender-flowered dress and slipped quickly out the kitchen door. Kumani was making tea, but she said she would just take a piece of toast and leave at once. She cranked the engine and roared off in a cloud of dust, not daring to glance back at her veranda as she passed. But she breathed a sigh of relief when she drove out of sight of her house.

She had to work hard to concentrate on the church service. Her mind kept slipping away to her veranda and the man who waited on it. It was a relief when she was finally sitting on the MacDougals' cool shady veranda, sipping a tall glass of orange juice.

Sarah told Ethel and Ralph all about Peter, and how he was the son of a doctor she knew and admired in Aberdeen. Lunch was served, and still Sarah talked. She explained how he had no one who could look after him in Nairobi and why he couldn't bear to stay at the hospital. She asked Ralph if he could contact the French mission and request that they take Mr. Stewart in. Everything she had been worrying about for the last two weeks came tumbling out. Everything except for her feelings for Peter. And when she was finally finished, she paused and said, "Thank you for listening to me. It's so good just to tell someone what has been going on, and I appreciate the two of you so much for listening."

Ralph stood up. "I suspect you two women would rather talk without a man around, so if you'll excuse me, I'll just go and lie down for my afternoon nap. But I'll be sure to send word to the French mission about Mr. Stewart first thing in the morning, Sarah." And he left them.

"Come, Sarah, let's walk," said Ethel, putting her arm through Sarah's. They stepped out into the garden, into a purple snowfall of mauve blossoms that drifted down around them as a breeze stirred through the big jacaranda tree that shaded the MacDougals' home.

"So, your young man is making a remarkable recovery, is he?" Ethel began, with a sly smile as her husband disappeared into the house.

"Ethel! Don't! He is not my young man."

"But, Sarah, you are blushing."

"That's only because you're teasing me, Ethel. And yes, he's determined to get better as quickly as he can. He is doing it too."

Ethel had stopped smiling. "He must be awfully grateful to his pretty young nurse for saving his life. Come, Sarah, tell me, don't you think it would be romantic if he fell in love with you, even a little bit?"

"It isn't he who is falling in love." There was a minute of silence while Sarah let Ethel think of the implications.

"But, my dear, is that such a bad thing? We all fall in love at least once in our lives. You are a vibrant young woman. You are bound to fall for a handsome young man like Peter. And I'd bet you dollars to doughnuts he's at least a little bit in love with you too. I very much doubt he could help himself!"

"But I don't think he is really a Christian. I mean, think he believes, the way most people believe in God, but I don't think he is really committed to faith in Jesus Christ. I can't possibly let anything happen between the two of us. It wouldn't be right."

Ethel sighed. "When Ralph and I met, I wasn't terribly committed to my faith either. But Ralph was the minister of our church, and I thought he was the most handsome man I had ever seen. After we got to know each other a little bit, he sat with me and explained everything. And when I heard the gospel spelled out so clearly that I could understand it, I believed too. If you do the same thing for Peter, I have no doubt that he will believe, just like I did. Perhaps he has never been told the gospel in a way that made sense to him. You know, many people go to church, but they don't actually hear what is being taught until someone sits them down and tells them one on one."

Sarah tried to imagine herself telling Peter about her faith. It made her feel shy and insecure. What if he laughed or, worse yet, was merely condescending? She remembered his bitter tone of voice when he spoke about his past. What if he became angry? But deep inside, she knew fear was a poor excuse for not sharing the gospel.

"Yes, you're right. I must talk to Peter before he leaves. But I don't think it will make him fall in love with me the way you did with Ralph. Anyway, I suppose he'll be gone, and that's the last I'll see of him!"

Ethel smiled. "You'd be surprised, my dear. God works in mysterious ways, you know."

Sarah shook her head. "I don't think so, Ethel. At least not in my case. My life is pretty plain and simple. But you're right about telling him the gospel before he leaves my house. That's the least I can do."

Sarah walked with Ethel for a little while longer, enjoying the chance to chat and listen to Ethel's problems and worries. It felt good to talk to someone about the everyday things that filled their lives. She had thought she was quite capable of living an isolated life, but now that Peter had burst into her world, she realized how lonely it was for her, living alone with only Kumani for company. She decided she would continue to keep up her new friendship with Ethel even after Peter left. At least her relationship with him had taught her this much.

When Sarah arrived home with the sun setting over the hills behind her, she found Peter walking around the garden, leaning on Kumani's shoulder. She was horrified!

"Peter Stewart! Get back into bed at once. How did you get down those steps? You will pull out all your stitches. Kumani, I told you he was not to get out of bed while I was gone!"

"Memsahib, I tried to tell him to stay in bed, but he wouldn't listen to me. He said he would go alone if I didn't help him. So I had to do something. I'm sorry!"

"That's all right, Kumani." She turned to Peter. "Into bed. This instant! You should be ashamed of yourself, making Kumani disobey me!"

Peter smiled sheepishly, "I'm sorry, Nurse. Please forgive me and help me back to my bed. I'm suddenly feeling a bit tired." He did look very pale. Sarah rushed over to take his other side. As he draped his arm over her shoulders and leaned his weight on her, Sarah felt the familiar shiver set her nerves aflutter. It was not entirely a disagreeable feeling either.

They reached the steps of the veranda. Peter stopped and said quietly, "I am afraid I should have listened to you. I don't think I can get up the steps. I can feel the stitches pulling."

"Oh dear, I hope you haven't already done any damage. Kumani, we will have to link our arms together, like this, and carry him." They reached underneath him, and between the two of them, panting and straining, they lifted his weight up the stairs and set him on the veranda. Then they half dragged and half carried him to the cot and carefully laid him down. Sarah collapsed in the chair beside the bed, puffing with the exertion of lifting his weight. Peter was lying with his eyes closed, his face white, and his breathing strained, as if he was trying not to move any of his muscles for fear of tearing his stitches.

"Sorry, Sarah," he said faintly. She looked over and saw that he had a new look of respect, perhaps, as he tried to smile for her. "My dad trained you very well. You have looked after me better than I deserve."

"Oh, nonsense!" Sarah was annoyed to feel a hot blush rushing into her cheeks. "I'd do the same for anyone."

"I know you would, Sarah. That's what makes you so special. But I will get better and make you glad you did all you did for me. I promise." And he closed his eyes.

Sarah turned and quickly went into the house in case he opened his eyes and saw her face. It was shining, she was sure of it. She rushed to the basin in the corner of her bedroom and rinsed her face until it was red from the scrubbing, not the blood rushing up from her wildly beating heart. *The sooner he leaves here the better!*

In the morning, as they sat together eating their breakfast in the moist, misty morning air, Sarah was quiet. She hadn't slept very well. Peter Stewart's eyes, the touch of his skin, the weight of his body, and especially the words he spoke to her, had filled her fevered mind until she felt she was overflowing with new feelings and uncontrollable emotions. Now she was tired, and she was afraid he would be able to tell just by looking at her the kind of things she was feeling for him. She ate silently.

Suddenly there was a squawking of chickens in the back of the house, and they heard Kumani talking to someone. A minute later, Kumani arrived on the veranda with a note. Sarah opened it. She looked at Peter. "The friars at the French mission say they will be pleased to have you stay with them until you are well enough to look after yourself," she said, folding the paper back up and reaching into her pocket for a sixpence for Kumani to give the messenger. "You'll be able to ride there with Mr. Oswald when he comes to interview you on Wednesday." Peter nodded, but Sarah noticed that he looked away quickly and didn't say anything else.

At last, as Kumani was taking away their plates and Sarah was about to get up to go, he spoke.

"You know, I've been wondering what brought you out here to the middle of Africa, Sarah. You must be awfully courageous to come and live in the bush by yourself. I don't know many women who could live this life you've chosen."

Sarah thought quickly. This was just the opening she needed if she was going to talk to Peter about her faith. And she certainly didn't have much time left to do it.

But suddenly she felt nervous and shy. Would he still think she was special? Would he still think she was courageous? Or would he simply write her off as a religious fanatic who was too blinded by her faith to make rational decisions? She suddenly, desperately wanted him to continue to think well of her. She didn't think she could bear it if he became condescending or patronizing, the way people often reacted back home when she told them of her plans.

She could always imagine their thoughts. "Oh, she's young and she's idealistic. Give her time, and if she isn't eaten by a lion or bitten by a snake, she'll come home and get married like any sensible girl. On the other hand, she isn't terribly attractive, so perhaps it is just as well she wants to be a missionary."

Sarah would smile a hard, bright smile and go on her way, but she always kept track in her heart of hearts about who had treated her this way. She knew it was wrong, but she was still not strong enough in her faith to overlook these slights. And it was terribly important just at this moment that Peter didn't become one of this group. She could feel Peter's smile on her, warm and accepting.

"Well, don't you want to tell me?" he asked.

"I'm just doing what God has called me to do," she blurted out quickly. She simply must plow ahead, or she might never get another chance. "Did you hear of Eric Liddell? He was the one who inspired me to go into missionary work."

"Ah, yes, Eric Liddell. The man who refused to run his race on a Sunday, even though he was in the Olympics. I remember him."

"He's a missionary now, serving in China. And he did run in the Olympics. He ran in another race, and he won a gold medal. He says God honors those who honor Him. He honored God by not running on a Sunday, and God honored him by helping him to win another race.

"I heard him speak about his faith in God. I was so impressed by how he wanted to really live out the calling that God has given us in the Bible to go out and make disciples of all nations. After all, what better gift could you give someone than the gift of knowing Jesus Christ and the promise of living with Him in heaven if you believe in Him? I realized that if I really loved Jesus, and I wanted to love Him, then the way to show it was to obey Him. So I decided to become a missionary. I didn't intend to come to Africa, though. I applied to go to China. But the Missionary Society assigned me to Africa. There's a greater need here at the moment than in China. So here I am."

There, she had done it. She hadn't flinched, even though she had been close to doing so. She was so relieved about this that she almost didn't hear Peter's next question.

"If the best gift you can give someone is to tell them about Jesus Christ, then why aren't you telling me? Don't I count?"

Sarah wasn't sure he was serious. She looked at him carefully, but his eyes were sincerely questioning. "Well, I, um, didn't think you were interested. Yet. After all, you have been rather ill."

"Exactly. What if I had died?"

Sarah didn't know what he was doing. Was he actually annoyed that she had not told him about her faith in Jesus?

"Would you like me to tell you about my faith now?"

His face opened into a wide smile. "I suppose I am just curious. I've never met a woman quite like you, Sarah. I've spent a lot of time lying flat on my back doing nothing. I'm not used to doing nothing, so I have been thinking about you. I just want to know what makes you tick."

Sarah suddenly felt irritated. "So I'm just a curiosity

to you then. Someone to think about because you have nothing else to do!"

"No! No, that's not what I meant at all! I really am intrigued by you. I honestly haven't ever met anyone like you before. And if you are doing all this because of your faith, then I want to know about a faith like yours. I have met many Christians, and none of them have done anything like this. Please don't be offended. I didn't mean it the wrong way."

"Oh. I suppose I was just a little surprised by your question." The worried look on his face when he thought he had upset her didn't hurt either. But she didn't want him to know that. So she told him about Jesus and what He meant to her. She told him how He was real, alive, and always communicating with her through His answers to her prayers. Peter knew all the old Bible stories. Everyone in Scotland learned them in school, but he thought that's all they were—just old stories.

"I'm not sure I can really believe the way you do, Sarah," he said at last, when she had finished. "But I do admire you for your conviction and your integrity. One day when I'm well, I am going to come back and see this clinic of yours. I sincerely hope and pray it is a success, although I know I'll never have faith like yours."

"I'll pray for you too, Peter." Sarah thought of Ethel's reason for praying for Peter's conversion. For a moment she hoped Ethel's prayers would be answered. But it was already midmorning, and in the hot glare of the sunlight on the red earth, romantic notions about this real, flesh- and-blood person in front of her seemed pretty far-fetched. "And now, I really had better go and get some work done on my building project." She rushed off, leaving Peter to watch her go.

When she returned for lunch, Peter was sitting up at the table, waiting for her. He carried on the conversation as if she had never left. He took a particular interest in everything to do with the construction of her clinic. He asked her many questions about how she intended it to function when it was built and what equipment she would need and what type of medical assistance she planned to give to the people in the vicinity. She found herself telling him about her plans, then about her hopes and even her dreams.

Her dream, she explained to him, was to build a clinic and show the missionary branch in Scotland that there was enough work out here for a doctor. Eventually she wanted to be able to build a hospital here. Her eyes flashed with determination as she described her ambitions to him as they sat on the veranda, watching the setting sun and waiting for Kumani to come out and light the lamps and bring supper. Peter never laughed. He took everything she said very seriously. He reminded her of his father back in the hospital in Aberdeen.

❧

That evening, after she had washed for supper, she sat on the veranda with Peter. As usual she was wearing her lavender-flowered dress. She was certain he liked it, since he always had a certain look of surprised admiration whenever she wore it. She had seen men look at women that way before, but this was the first time anyone looked at her this way. And she had to admit that she liked the flush of pleasure she felt with Peter's gaze on her. She must also admit that she was going to miss him an awful lot when he left. Their conversation today was making her feel confident and secure enough that she thought she could ask him something.

"Peter, tell me. What is it about the Christian faith that you don't like?"

He paused for a moment, considering the question. "I just saw too much suffering during the war, that's all," he replied. "I don't see how God could leave so many men to suffer and die so horribly and not do anything about it. I just came to the conclusion that He didn't care."

Sarah had not forgotten the bitterness he had shown when he spoke about his brother's death. She heard it in his voice again now. He was a man who had the courage to face his own physical pain and overcome it, but emotional pain seemed to be too much for him to cope with. He needed to know that God's love was real, even in the midst of emotional suffering. But how could she talk about suffering to a man who had seen so much more of it than she had? On the other hand, how could she not reply to his comment that God just didn't care? She had to say something.

"Oh, Peter, it must have been a terrible ordeal for you!" That was not exactly what she had meant to say, and certainly she had not meant to speak so passionately.

Peter turned to her. He looked directly into her eyes. "Yes, it was terrible, worse than terrible." He turned away again. "Soldiers are expected to keep a stiff upper lip and just get on with their jobs: the killing and the dying. No feelings, no pain. But it isn't like that. It is a terrible thing to watch people suffer and pray desperately, then die anyway. And no one can do a blessed thing for them. Not even God."

"But how do you know God didn't care or didn't do

anything about it? I nursed soldiers who came back from the war, and they told me about praying to God to save their lives. And He did. They believed that it was a miracle they were saved, while everyone around them died."

"Everyone around them died." Peter repeated her words. "Why didn't God save the others too? Weren't they good enough? People like my brother died in terrible pain. I prayed to God to stop his suffering, and all that happened was that he died. He was a Christian too, you know."

"But Peter, if he was a Christian, then he is no longer suffering. You must see that! God did answer your prayer."

"Sure, at my expense and my father's expense and my mother's too. No, Sarah, I just can't believe in a God who would allow so many people to suffer so much and do nothing to stop it. I'm sorry."

Sarah didn't know how to answer Peter. It seemed to her that arguments on the existence of God were missing the point of what was really upsetting him. She suspected that even if she were mathematically able to prove that God was real, it would still not be enough. Bitterness and anger like Peter's stemmed from a deeper cause. She would need to pray for him.

Peter sat in his chair now, breathing hard with the exertion of his speech. Or perhaps with the exertion of his feelings. He looked up at her at last. "But there is one thing I need to admit to you, though, if I am to be completely truthful." He paused. "When that rhino was charging me, I prayed. Yes, I prayed then, but I am ashamed to admit it. I didn't pray when it was charging

Jock, I was only thinking of my gun and whether I was aiming for the right place to kill the beast. But when it came at me, like a coward, I prayed then. Perhaps if I had prayed for Jock while I had had the chance, he would be alive today. If I had prayed for him instead of me, it might be him sitting here with you, not me.

"As soon as I am better, I am going to go and apologize to his widow. If God were as good as you say He is, He would have let me die instead of Jock. He has someone here who needs him, and I have no one, not one person who needs me. Yet I am living and Jock is dead. Where is the sense in that?"

"I don't know, Peter. I cannot explain everything God chooses to do. I only know that He is real and that He loves us. Perhaps, even now, He is comforting Jock's widow. Perhaps He knows things about Jock that we have no idea about. We with our small, finite minds cannot know the mind of God. But I do know this: God does exist, and He sent His own Son to die for our sins. That is real love."

"I don't know, Sarah. I've heard all the arguments for God's existence and His love before. I just can't bring myself to believe them, that's all. But I do admire people like you who have such genuine faith. Anyway, I don't want to talk about it anymore. I'm tired."

Sarah sighed. "Yes, it's late. Mr. Oswald will be here bright and early, and you will have a long day traveling, so you had better get some rest. I'll say good night."

She got up and helped him out of his chair. They walked over to his bed, and Sarah found herself thinking that this would be the last time she would feel the weight of him on her shoulder. When they reached the bed,

Peter stopped. Sarah looked at him, and again he leaned forward and kissed her cheek. "Thank you for everything, Sarah. Thank you for my life," he whispered, then let go of her and sank onto the bed.

Sarah called Kumani to help Peter get ready for bed. Then she went into the bedroom and flung herself on the bed. She wanted to cry. She told herself she was being too emotional and far too unprofessional, but the tears trickled down her face anyway, and a minute later she found herself sobbing into her pillow.

Much later that night, when her emotions were spent, Sarah knew she ought to pray for him. "But, Lord," she whispered into the blackness, "I don't want to pray for him. You know how he makes me feel. I am falling in love with him. I need to forget him, Lord, not pray for him. But I'll pray for him tonight, then please release me from my responsibility to him."

Tuesday was a long day, and she avoided Peter as much as possible. When they were together at mealtimes, they also avoided the subject of God. Whether it was intentional on his part or not, Sarah didn't know. But Peter was leaving tomorrow, and even though she had prayed for release from a responsibility for him, he was in her thoughts. Even while she tried to sleep, she couldn't help recalling their conversation about God and how she had fallen in love with Peter Stewart.

It was a long night, and Sarah slept off and on, dreaming and waking without really being able to tell which was which.

In the morning, when she came onto the veranda, she found Peter standing looking out onto the pink western hills, with the remains of his safari—two guns and a pistol—packed at his feet. Mr. Oswald arrived about half an hour later in his large black car. Peter and Sarah stood and watched the red herald of dust approaching.

"Peter Stewart?" Mr. Oswald bounced up the veranda steps in two strides. "Good, I see you're ready to go. I'm in a bit of a hurry this morning. I need to make a stop in Kisumu as soon as possible. Had a bit of trouble on one of the farms up that way. Morning, Miss Cameron. Sorry I must be rushing off and can't stay for a cuppa." He motioned for his driver to come and help with Peter's luggage. Sarah put out her arm to help Peter down the steps, but he put his arm around her shoulders the way he had done when he first walked after the accident.

"Listen, Sarah, I am sorry about some of the things I said the other night. I owe my very life to you."

"Nonsense!" Sarah interrupted, but she couldn't meet his eyes.

"Thank you for all you've done for me, Sarah. I am truly grateful." They were at the bottom of the steps. He bent forward and kissed her on the cheek. She could feel his soft lips brushing her skin, and then she heard him whisper, "I'll be back soon. Look out for me." She could feel Mr. Oswald watching them. She could hardly raise her eyes to look at him.

"Good-bye, Peter," she stammered, as she helped him into the car.

"Cheerio!" called Mr. Oswald, as he put his foot to the floor and roared off down the road.

Sarah stood watching the red cloud rise into the blue sky. She could only feel a dark aching void where a moment ago her heart had been beating so hard.

Kumani was standing on the veranda when Sarah

turned to go back inside.

"Well, that's that," she said to him, and instead of going out to the clinic, she threw herself into her big chair, the one Peter had always used. Kumani went back inside. She felt tired and empty. She felt as though she didn't want to do anything at all but sit here and remember the last couple of weeks.

But there were a lot of things to do. There were letters to write, shopping to do. She hadn't been to Nairobi for weeks, and she wanted to get a few more supplies at the hospital. Also, there were some things she needed for the building. She should really plan a trip. It would be good to go and talk to Dr. Mainwaring about some of the cases she was seeing in the clinic that she was perplexed about. And she should also check in at the mission office to make a report, now that the clinic was becoming a real entity.

But she couldn't move. She wondered how Peter was coping with the bumpy car ride. She hoped Mr. Oswald wouldn't have to spend too much time in Kisumu. It was going to be a long trip for Peter in his condition, without having to wait for hours for Mr. Oswald to get his business done.

The house already seemed quiet and lonely without Peter. It would take some getting used to, the way she'd had to get used to the loneliness of the place when she first came. The touch of his kiss still lingered on her cheek. It was the beginning of a new loneliness for Sarah, such as she had never known before.

five

After Peter left, Sarah's days went on as they had before she had ever laid eyes on him. They were filled with the work of healing the people who came to her. She spent as much time as she could supervising the constructing of her new clinic building. The foundation was being laid, and many trees had to be cut and stripped for the building.

But the joy and the anticipation that she felt in her work had vanished into thin air like the dust from the car that took Peter Stewart back to Nairobi. She often caught herself looking down the road as if he might just appear again, roaring back in a cloud of dust the way he had left. She longed to be able to put him out of her mind forever, but her will was just not strong enough to overcome her feelings about him. The days and the nights were lonely and difficult, and Sarah found that she couldn't even pour out her heart to God the way she used to. Peter always came to mind whenever she tried to pray.

Sarah had been putting off the trip to Nairobi to order supplies for the new clinic because she didn't have the energy to pretend to be happy and hopeful when she saw everyone at the mission headquarters. But it would take months for the equipment and the medicine to arrive by ship, and by then she hoped her clinic would be built. So, finally, she could delay no more.

The trip to Nairobi took Sarah and Kumani half a day, most of it over rough, bumpy roads. But apart from the usual bumps and detours around fallen logs or washed-out streams, it was uneventful.

Sarah arrived late in the morning at the missionary headquarters, which was located in a large old house on a shady, tree-lined street. She sat in the roomy old lounge of the house and looked around at the soft couches and Persian rugs on the floor.

Anita Webster, the secretary and receptionist, ordered tea for the two of them. She was a pretty, round-faced girl with curly brown hair and a light, sunny smile. Sarah smiled at her. She had just the kind of personality to keep the office running cheerfully, welcoming missionaries who hadn't seen civilization for months and making them feel right at home.

While they were waiting for tea, Anita quickly caught Sarah up on all the local gossip and chatted about the news from the other missionaries in the country. But as soon as the tea tray was set before them, Anita suddenly changed the subject. She leaned forward and said, "So, Sarah, tell me your news. I've been hearing all sorts of stories. They say you saved the life of that poor man who was gored by a rhino, and he stayed at your house for nearly a month. What was his name, Peter Stewart? My goodness, Sarah, people are talking. Tell me what really happened!"

"Anita, he was unconscious most of the time. And I didn't even know who he was."

"Ooh, it sounds so romantic! I want to hear all about it."

"What do you mean, people are talking, Anita? Who is talking? About what?"

"Kenya is a small place, and news gets around. Especially about an attractive and lonely young missionary who saves the life of a handsome safari guide, who stays with her alone in the wilderness while he recovers."

Sarah was at a loss for words. What if people suspected that she really had fallen in love with Peter Stewart? She would simply die of shame and embarrassment. That thought jolted her into action. "But, Anita, it was not romantic at all. The man almost died. He was delirious with fever for a good part of the time. And then he left. That's all there is to it." She almost added that Peter hadn't even sent her a thank-you note, but stopped herself, afraid that her real disappointment might show and give away her feelings for Peter.

"So, you really did save his life, then?" Anita asked. "Tell me everything! What is Peter Stewart like? No one seems to know much about him around here. But since the accident, everyone's talking. Some people say he was careless. Other people are saying it wasn't his fault, it was the gun bearer's fault. Others are convinced it was just a plain accident because, after all, rhinos are so unpredictable. What is the real story?"

"I don't really know. Peter can't remember too much of what happened. He didn't talk about it a lot, but he is very upset about the whole thing. He does think, though, that whatever happened, it was his fault because he was in charge."

"Poor man! He's riddled with guilt, then?"

"Well, I wouldn't call it exactly riddled," Sarah replied with a chuckle. Anita could find drama in everything, from having tea to being gored by rhinos. It was a talent. "He is naturally upset, and he's trying to think it all through carefully. When someone is killed, you always have to wonder if you could possibly have prevented it, especially if it's on your safari. But the district commissioner is looking into it, and I'm sure they will get to the bottom of it. I doubt Peter will be found to be lacking in his safety measures. He seems very responsible, even courageous, to me. I'm sure the whole story will come out soon enough."

Anita looked a little disappointed. "Well, were you shocked when they brought him to you?" she asked instead. "They're saying you saved his life. He must be terribly grateful to you if he owes you his very life. What was it like? Were you afraid he was going to die?"

Sarah told her the whole story, downplaying the drama of the situation as much as she could. She knew when Anita retold it, she would add the drama herself, and Sarah wanted to keep it as mundane as possible so as not to give her a head start.

They finished their tea, and Sarah stood up to go. She had people to see about getting the supplies she needed to furnish the clinic, and she wanted to see Dr. Mainwaring too. "Have you heard from Mr. Stewart since he arrived in Nairobi?" Anita asked her quickly.

"No."

Anita looked disappointed again for a moment. "That is a pity. I hoped he would be more loyal to you."

"Loyal? What do you mean? Why should he be loyal?" But Sarah's heart dropped into the pit of her stomach. Anita's words sent a chill through her.

"Well, you're the one who saved his life, but I hear stories of how he is seeing an awful lot of Jock Davis's widow." Anita lowered her voice ominously as she said this.

Sarah was confused. "So what? He doesn't have to

answer to me. And he said he had no friends. It is good for him to make new friends. He needs them."

"Not Ruby Davis's crowd. They're trouble." Anita snorted. "He needs friends like those people about as much as he needs another rhino to gore him. They are very bad news. They like to drink and gamble and have huge parties that last for days at a time. And it was such a romantic story, you saving his life and all, I was just hoping he was in love with you, and you could save him from that crowd."

Sarah felt as though she had been slapped. But really, for Anita to think that Peter Stewart would fall in love with her was ridiculous. The fact that she actually had fallen in love with him was another matter.

"Well, he isn't a Christian, Anita. You can't possibly think I would involve myself in a love affair with a man who doesn't love Jesus."

"No, no, of course not! But perhaps with you saving his life, he might just decide to become a Christian. It would have been so romantic, don't you think?"

Sarah wished Anita would stop talking this way. She was flustered that Anita had pinpointed her feelings about Peter so easily, so she laughed and said, "Anita, you should write love stories. But seriously, perhaps Peter Stewart needs prayer. Why don't you pray for him? I told him about Jesus, but he wouldn't listen. He's too bitter about all the suffering he saw during the war to believe that God loves people."

"I am praying for him. Our whole church has been praying for his recovery and his conversion ever since we learned about his accident and that you were the one who was looking after him."

Sarah put her teacup firmly on the tray and stood up. "I really must go and get a few things done before I run out of time. I don't want to get home too late tonight. Thanks for the tea and the chat, Anita. It's always nice to visit with you and catch up on all the news."

"Good-bye, Sarah. Remember to pray for Peter too!"

Sarah waved as she walked out to the street, where Kumani was waiting in the lorry. She didn't want to pray for Peter, as it would only make her think about him more. What she really wanted was to put him out of her life.

Sarah drove down to the main road. African women, carrying huge loads of vegetables or jars of water on their heads, stalked regally down the street. Sarah always marveled at their skill. Horses and cars churned down the middle of the road, stirring the dust up while little totos darted here and there in between, chasing chickens and goats to the market. Sarah made her way to the hospital. She would order a few medical supplies and visit Dr. Mainwaring.

Secretly, she wondered if she might bump into Peter somewhere. Nairobi was not a big place, and Peter was probably still under doctor's care, even if he was not staying in the hospital itself. She had thought she could ask Dr. Mainwaring about how he was getting on, but she was afraid to go and visit Peter herself. Anyway, she might bump into him accidentally. . . .

But now the thought of accidentally bumping into him set her nerves on edge so badly she decided to sneak in the back of the hospital, through the kitchen entrance. She left Kumani with the lorry, parked in a dusty yard overrun with chickens and a goat or two.

Sarah slipped unnoticed through the kitchen, which was bustling at full speed to get lunches out to the patients. When she reached Dr. Mainwaring's office, he was just going out the door so he quickly invited her to have lunch with him out under the jacaranda trees in the hospital gardens.

Dr. Mainwaring sat down in a large wicker chair, and Sarah sat opposite him. "I was very impressed with the job you did stitching up Peter Stewart," he said, as they waited for the food to arrive. "He owes you his life, you know."

"Actually, it was his very own father who taught me how to do it. Did you ever hear of Dr. George Stewart of Aberdeen? I trained under him."

"Really! Well, it is a small world, isn't it?"

Sarah nodded. They chatted on about people they had both known back in Scotland, and about medical problems that Sarah was encountering among the Africans who came to her for treatment. At last, just before it was time for Dr. Mainwaring to return to work, Sarah quickly slipped in a question about Peter. She hoped she sounded nonchalant.

"Ah, yes, I meant to tell you earlier. He is recovering nicely. You did a bang-up job of sewing him back together, my dear. Although I sometimes get the impression that he wishes he had been in Jock Davis's place. He is taking risks with his health, I fear."

"Taking risks? What do you mean? He was so anxious to recover as quickly as possible when he was at my house. I couldn't get him to sit still. All he wanted to do was get back on his feet as soon as he could!"

"Really? Hmm." Dr. Mainwaring shook his head,

puzzled. "Well, it could be that he's feeling guilty about Jock's death. He was clearly hung over from a night of drinking when he was last in for a checkup. He looked peaked and thin. But there was nothing wrong with his wounds. They were coming along very nicely.

"Anyway, I must get back to my patients, Miss Cameron. It has been a pleasure to see you. Good luck with your clinic. It will be a tremendous help to the people out that way when you are up and running with it! And it will take a bit of the pressure off the hospital here too. Good day, Miss Cameron!"

Sarah watched him walk back to the hospital, thinking that she still needed to go to the hospital office and give them her list of supplies. She was not looking forward to the long drive home after that. She decided to sit for a moment in the peace and the shade of the garden and absorb the news she had gathered about Peter this morning. It sounded bad. Perhaps if she had put aside her selfish thoughts and prayed for the poor man, he would be doing better. She decided she had better repent and pray. She bent her head and was doing just that when someone startled her.

"Hallo! Is that you, Sarah? Don't tell me you are in Nairobi and you haven't bothered to come and see me!"

Sarah looked up into the familiar blue eyes of Peter Stewart. Her heart leaped in her breast while she desperately tried to look casually pleased to see him. "Oh, Peter! What are you doing here?" she stammered, noticing that he did not look particularly well. Dr. Mainwaring had been right about him. In fact, he had looked better just after he had recovered from his fever than he did now. His face was drawn and sallow, and he looked as though he was fighting a headache. He was also accompanied by a tiny, sharp-faced woman with lots of dark hair and bright red lipstick. Sarah smiled politely at her.

"I was just going to ask you that," he replied. "Sarah, may I introduce you to Ruby Davis. Ruby, this is Sarah Cameron."

"Oh, I am so pleased to meet you at last! Peter has told me so much about you, Miss Cameron. Everyone says you saved his very life. You must be so talented and so dedicated to live out there in the wilds and help the natives the way you do. Peter told me what wonderful work you do out there. In fact, he never seems to stop talking about you at all. He makes me quite jealous!" She tossed her thick black hair over her shoulder.

"Thank you," Sarah mumbled. So this was the grieving widow. She would have never guessed it if she had met her on the street. Instantly she was embarrassed by her own rude thoughts. Quickly she turned to Peter.

"How are you feeling, Peter? I'm only in town for one day, and I have so much to do. I thought I would try to look you up when I have a little more time to visit," she said, feeling guilty. He was looking down warmly at her, not really upset. Oh, but it felt so nice to be looking into his smiling face again. Her heart was repeating the old familiar flutter. It was as though nothing had changed in her feelings about him.

"Come and have tea with us, Sarah. I just came here to pick up some medication, and then we're off to the Lord Stanley Hotel for a drink. But you could have tea. Do come!" He was pleading. Sarah was sorely tempted. But she took a look at the hard smile on his companion's face, and she resisted.

"Thank you, Peter, but I must start heading home. My lorry is so unreliable, and I want to get as much of the trip done before dark. I hate being out in the dark."

"Alright, I suppose you had better get on your way, then. We'll walk over to the lorry with you. I'd like to say hello to Kumani too."

They started off across the lawn. Mrs. Davis—Ruby, as he called her—put her arm through his and helped him walk. Sarah could see he still had a bit of his limp. He did look tired too, as Dr. Mainwaring had said. Was he depressed as well? But Sarah found herself feeling too jealous of Mrs. Davis to think about Peter's feelings for long. She was the one who should be walking with Peter, not Ruby Davis. Sarah remembered the feel of Peter's weight on her shoulders as she supported him when he was so ill, and suddenly she ached to feel his arm around her again. Seeing Ruby Davis there in her place was almost unbearable.

Mrs. Davis was nattering away. Sarah forced herself to pay attention. It was a good thing she did, because suddenly Ruby turned to her and said, "Don't you think so, Miss Cameron?"

"Oh, yes, I mean, no!" Sarah replied, realizing that Mrs. Davis had just commented how terribly dangerous it was to be a lone woman in the African bush. "No, it's perfectly safe if you have a gun to shoot snakes with and if you have good relations with the Africans who live in the vicinity. I'm fortunate enough to have both," she announced firmly. But Mrs. Davis was not deterred.

"Peter, you must agree with me. Surely a woman all alone out there is a sitting duck for any native who wants to attack her without warning. I think Miss Cameron is very brave to live all alone like that. Of course, now that I have met you, Miss Cameron, I see you are as tall as a man and probably as strong. But you are still a woman, so I give you credit for bravery. And, of course, you are a missionary, so God is watching over you too. I can see why Peter admires you so much. Don't you, Peter?"

"Excuse me, Ruby, I wasn't listening." Sarah noticed that Peter had been watching her over the top of Ruby's head and wasn't paying attention to Ruby either. It made her feel slightly better.

They had reached the lorry. Peter chatted with Kumani, and then he and Sarah began a conversation about the progress of her clinic. Mrs. Davis became bored. She wandered over to where some patients were strolling by and began to chat with them.

Suddenly Peter lowered his voice. "Why didn't you let me know you were in town, Sarah? I would have taken you out to lunch."

"Peter, I really was only here for a quick business trip to order some things for the clinic. Besides, I hadn't heard from you, so I wasn't sure how to reach you."

"But I wrote to you the very day I got here. Didn't you get my letter?

"No." Sarah looked away, afraid of meeting Peter's eyes. She had heard so many odd things about him today, she wasn't sure she believed him, anyway.

"Sarah!" He took her by the shoulders and looked right into her eyes. "You must have thought I didn't even have the decency to thank you for all you did for me! I am so sorry. But I sent you a letter, and I asked you to keep me informed about how your clinic was progressing. I never heard a word from you. I thought you weren't interested in keeping in touch with me!"

As Sarah looked into his face, she knew he was telling the truth. Relief broke over her like a wave, and she smiled. He swallowed as if he were nervous and said gruffly, "So, would you mind if I paid you a visit one of these days?"

"No, I'd be delighted." Sarah's voice was barely a whisper. "You are always welcome."

"I'll count on it."

Kumani was turning the crank to try and start the lorry. Suddenly it roared to life, and Peter leaned forward and kissed Sarah on the cheek again. Quickly she turned to get into the cab. She caught a glimpse of Mrs. Davis walking over toward them. She had seen the kiss, and she didn't look very happy.

"Good-bye, Peter."

"See you soon, Sarah." He gave her a little salute at the top of his forehead. Was it her imagination, or did his smile seem a little brighter? Mrs. Davis arrived and took him firmly by the arm as Kumani pulled away from them.

"I'm so tired, Kumani," Sarah said. "I think I'll just sleep for a few minutes before the road gets rough." She needed the privacy of her own thoughts, which were swirling wildly out of her control. Over and over again, Sarah relived the soft touch of Peter's lips on her cheeks. Was this really what being in love felt like? Whatever it was, there was something there that defied her rational will. Did he feel it too? Why did he kiss her cheek again? Surely he wasn't just being old-fashioned and gallant. Why was he so upset she hadn't let him know she would be in town today? Was it because everyone said she had saved his life and he wanted to show her he was very grateful? Or was it because he genuinely liked being with her?

Sarah's thoughts turned to Ruby Davis. Was she just being a friend and helping with his recovery? Sarah couldn't bring herself to believe that. Was Peter Stewart in love with Jock Davis's widow? If he was, why did he want to come and see her so much?

Sarah, that's enough!

It didn't matter what Peter Stewart thought about her. He was not hers to have. He was not God's to give her. Anita was praying, but that was just romantic Anita. And Ethel was too.

Ethel! She would go and talk to Ethel and tell her everything she had seen and heard today. She needed to tell someone, or she would simply go mad.

And she had better start praying too. But not about Peter. She could leave that to Anita. She would pray for her own heart and mind. She needed to pray that God would take control of her feelings so that she didn't fall into sin by falling in love with someone who did not love God. God, who had promised to help the weak, would have to help her with this dilemma. She set her mind to praying for strength and pure thoughts. Now and then, however, her mind wandered, and she found herself feeling the warmth of his kiss on her cheek, but she knew God would answer her prayers for help sooner or later. The sooner the better. She had better continue to pray for patience too.

six

Sarah worked hard when she got back home. The clinic was coming along faster now that the heavy clearing and the foundation was finished. Every day she supervised its progress. In the evenings she worked on her correspondence and reread her medical books. Each night she dropped into bed as exhausted as she could possibly make herself. One night as she waited for sleep, praying as she always did, Sarah ruefully thanked God for sending Peter into her life. After all, she admitted, keeping her mind off him had had a marvelous effect. She had accomplished so much more than she ever would have done at her usual pace. "Lord, it is exhausting, though," she sighed and fell asleep.

But in the mornings, as she worked with the sick and wounded that came to her for help, she realized that she was not being completely honest with herself. Each time someone walked into her yard, she caught herself looking up to see if it was Peter.

One morning, she was bandaging a little toto who had accidentally slipped and burned his leg in the family's cooking fire. The boy was whining and crying while his mother held him close on her lap. It took all Sarah's attention to get the actual burn area covered with the bandage as he tried to pull his leg away each time she came near it.

"Here, let me help you," a voice said right behind her.

Sarah nearly jumped right out of her skin, and the toto screamed as she pressed too hard on his wound. "Oh, I'm sorry I frightened you, Sarah!"

"Peter Stewart! What are you doing here? How dare you sneak up and frighten me like that!" Sarah's heart was beating hard, but at least there was a good reason for it this time! The little boy howled.

"Forgive me, I didn't mean it." Peter was already kneeling down in an attempt to calm the boy, which he did with amazing skill, Sarah noticed. She bent down too, and they finished the job together. Sarah's hands were shaking. She blamed it on the fright he had given her.

"Well, how nice to see you again, Peter," she said, as soon as she had finished giving instructions to the mother on how to keep the wound clean and dry.

"It's wonderful to be back, Sarah. It almost feels like I'm coming home. I'll help you with the rest of your patients, and then perhaps you would be good enough to invite me for a bite of lunch."

She found Peter amazingly helpful. "You have a doctor's hands, like your father," she said as he held a feverish little baby for her while she examined her throat and ears and eyes. He didn't reply.

Lunch was late because the patients had taken longer than usual. Kumani had it waiting on the table behind them when they were finished. Sarah went inside to wash and came back out to find Peter sitting in his usual chair, chatting with Kumani as though he had never left. A wave of joy shivered down her spine, and she smiled happily as she sat down beside Peter.

"Well?" she said.

"Well, what?"

"Well, how are you feeling? You look well. Much better than you were when I saw you in Nairobi."

"Why, Miss Cameron, I didn't realize you were still taking such a proprietary interest in my case," he teased.

"Of course, I am," she said, blushing as she tried to speak casually. "And you've done very well to get better so quickly, Mr. Stewart."

"Why, thank you very much. I do feel a little weak still, but I can only be grateful for the excellent medical care I have received."

"And how is Mrs. Davis? She seemed to be taking her husband's death very well." Sarah couldn't resist the urge to bring up Ruby Davis, especially under the cover of teasing.

"She's doing well too. Thank you for asking. Next time I see her, I'll tell her you inquired after her."

They were sitting together, not eating. He was clearly waiting for her to say grace. She bowed her head. "Thank you, Lord, for the food You have provided us with today, and the friends You have given to share it with. Amen." It was short and sweet, but Sarah was feeling too flustered to think of anything more.

"Did you walk here all the way from Gilgil?" she asked.

"Yes, I took the early train. I thought that if you don't mind, I'd spend the night on your veranda. For old times' sake." His eyes twinkled, and Sarah was too glad to see him again to disapprove of his staying overnight at her house.

As they ate, she told him all the details, the triumphs, and the difficulties she was having building the clinic. She had been waiting to hear about the arrival of her supplies in Nairobi, she explained. And as she chatted on, she kept looking at him, trying to discern his motive for coming out to see her. But he was inscrutable. He just listened and asked questions occasionally.

Finally, as they sat in the quiet of the afternoon, empty plates before them, Sarah opened her mouth to say, "What are you doing here?" but at the last second she lost her courage. "How is Mr. Oswald coming along with the investigation of the accident?" she asked instead.

"He's written the whole thing up as an unfortunate accident caused by an accidental discharge of a firearm due to inexperience on the part of my gun bearer, Juma, combined with the volatile nature of rhinoceri, in general."

Sarah smiled as Peter imitated the bureaucratic language of the governmental services. Peter was clearly doing his best to be charming. And it was working.

"Well, I suppose you will be going back into the safari business, then?"

He smiled at her for a moment before answering. "Yes, I think I will. I don't really have much choice, I suppose. I could take up farming, but I'm a city boy and don't know the first thing about growing things or raising livestock. And I would be bored to tears working in the bank or the government."

After lunch, they sat together chatting about this and that, until Peter asked her if she would take him out to the clinic. Sarah obliged, and they spent the afternoon there. He had brought a walking stick with him in case he got tired. But strolling back along the path in the late-afternoon shadows, Sarah found herself remembering the walks they had taken as he had leaned on her for support. She suddenly wished he could do it once more, casually, as if it were the most easy thing in the world, just drape his arm over her and walk with her into the sunset. For a minute the feeling was so strong it felt like an actual physical ache. She tried to brush it away by telling herself it was just the "chemistry" people spoke of.

She and Peter had supper together that evening. It felt to Sarah as if he had never left. They watched the sun go down and sat by the light of the hurricane lamp in the darkness, listening to the night insects and the frogs. The stars were flung out across the black sky like drops of shining happiness, scattered to the four corners of the heavens.

The joy of the Lord. They show off God's joy in the work of His creation.

"Sarah," Peter began suddenly.

"Yes," she replied, suddenly afraid. She had never heard him use that tone of voice.

"I did not come all this way just to pay you a friendly visit. I had another reason."

She looked up into his face in amazement. "What is it?"

"Oh, Sarah, this is so difficult for me to say. I'm really not used to talking about these things. And I am afraid I really don't understand women very well at all."

Sarah chuckled and said, "Women aren't that difficult to understand, Peter. Just say what you want to say. I'm sure if you put it in plain English, I'll understand you perfectly." *Goodness gracious, men were very odd. What on earth could Peter possibly want from me that makes him so terribly nervous?*

"Alright, then," he replied and took a deep breath. "Sarah, will you marry me?"

"What!" Sarah jumped up out of her chair. "Peter! What are you talking about?"

Peter stood up too. He took her by the hands and said, "But, Sarah, you said you would understand me if I just put it in plain English."

"But. . .but. . ." Sarah was speechless. He was standing close to her, looking into her eyes as if he were trying to read the very thoughts inside her head. Only there were no thoughts to read. There was simply the "Yes!" that every fiber of her being was shouting.

He must have heard it because he leaned forward and took her in his arms and kissed her. She melted into his arms, and time stood still while Sarah felt the warmth and passion of his kiss flood through her body. She loved it. And when they parted, they stood looking at each other like they were the first two people on the face of the whole earth. He moved forward to take her in his arms again, but it was a mistake. The spell he had woven around her was broken.

"No. No, Peter." She stepped backward and stumbled into her chair. She let herself fall into it.

"Sarah, please." Now he was down on one knee, kneeling in front of her. "Please don't say no until you've given it more thought."

Sarah stood up again. "No. Peter, you are not a Christian." Her mind was clearing at last. "I can't marry someone who doesn't love God." She turned away. The bougainvillea was blowing in the breeze, and Sarah walked toward it. It was the first thing she had planted in her new home. She had brought the cutting from Nairobi because when she was a little girl she had read about bougainvillea in a storybook, and she wanted one

of her own. Her bougainvillea was growing and bloom-
ing, and it was a powerful reminder to her of the life and
work God had given her here. She picked a tissue blos-
som and turned around. Peter had followed her.

"I've thought of that," he said, putting his hands on
her shoulders and looking deeply into her eyes. Sarah
felt she could hardly breathe, but he was talking quietly
and earnestly, "I know that if you give me time I'll
study the Bible. I promise I will do whatever it takes to
become a Christian so that I can marry you." He was
speaking quickly now, as though he didn't want her to
say no before he could get all his arguments in.

"I can help you too. I'll use this as the base for my
safaris. Safaris are big business these days, and I can
make money and invest it into the work you are doing
here. Perhaps, sooner rather than later, we'll have
enough to start building a real hospital. Just think of all
the good you can do. . .all the good we can do together.
Please, Sarah, don't say no. I love you, Sarah, and I
think we'd make a good team. If we bring our resources
and talents together, we'll both get where we want to
go. At least give yourself some time to think it over
before you give me an answer!"

Sarah couldn't believe she was hearing this. She was
shocked and appalled. He was promising to become a
Christian so that he could marry her. How could he
think such a thing! And as if having access to his money
would make her agree to it. How could he possibly
imagine she was so shallow and so greedy? The shock
and turmoil of Peter's surprise was rapidly turning into
fury in Sarah's heart.

"Peter, it sounds to me like you want to marry me as a

business arrangement. You say you love me, but you don't know the first thing about me if you don't know the God I serve."

"Sarah—"

"No," she repeated, really angry now. "How dare you? Marry you for the money you make! And then you will do me the favor of turning into a Christian! May God strike me with lightening if I should ever even think of accepting your offer. How dare you!"

"That isn't what I mean, Sarah, and you know it. You know I love you. You women know these things long before we men even have the first clue. So don't act surprised and hoity-toity. I am just trying to take the practical approach here. But I see now how wrong I was. All you want is the mushy stuff about loving God and loving you and romantically going off to foreign lands to save the souls of the lost. Well, forget it! And by the way, I noticed you didn't have a particular aversion to kissing me either. I didn't exactly receive a slap across my face, did I?"

Sarah couldn't believe her ears. How did things get this bizarre so quickly? Peter was pacing back and forth across the veranda. Suddenly she wanted him to be gone. She would deal with the aftermath of this appalling scene later when she had composed herself. But first she must get rid of Peter. With a conscious effort she controlled her voice and said, "Leave. Leave this minute. I don't care where you go. Take my lorry if you like. Just get out!"

He picked up his walking stick and disappeared into the darkness. She stood and watched the darkness until she was sure he was not coming back. Then she turned, ran into the house, and threw herself onto her bed. She cried painful, deep, racking sobs, until she thought her lungs would surely burst out of her body.

A long time later, when she was utterly spent, she suddenly felt it was terribly important that no one know what had happened. If no one knew, then it never happened. Life could continue in its usual placid, practical way, as though bizarre encounters in the night with strange men never, ever occurred. If only she could erase the whole experience from her mind.

Sarah spent the rest of the night praying. She begged God to remove the memory from her mind. She begged him to erase Peter from her heart. She begged to just go back to her simple old self, the self she was before she had ever met Peter. "It is a simple request, and surely You could answer me soon, Lord," she prayed. "Please answer my prayer quickly."

seven

Sarah woke up early the next morning and was dressed before Kumani brought in her tea. Leaving him in charge of the building work for the day, she set out for Gilgil. She had reconsidered Peter's proposal in the morning light and realized that she needed to go and tell Ethel MacDougal what had happened. She simply could not try to pretend it had never occurred. Her mind and heart and soul were in turmoil, and she couldn't even pray sensibly. All she could think of asking God, over and over again, was to take this problem away from her and let her be the way she was before she met Peter. She needed help, and she prayed that the MacDougals had not gone out for the day in their motorbike and sidecar.

But as Sarah pulled up to their house, she saw them sitting together on the veranda having coffee. She breathed a huge sigh of relief as she shut off the motor, and a moment later she was on the veranda, sitting in a chair and sipping a steaming cup of coffee herself.

"Well, Sarah, to what do we owe the pleasure of your visit this morning?" Ralph asked cheerfully.

Sarah hesitated. It would be difficult enough to explain what had happened to Ethel, and she didn't know if she could tell Ralph as well. But Ralph sensed her hesitation and immediately drained his coffee cup. "I am a married man, and I know when women don't need me around, so I'll just excuse myself. I believe I have a sermon to write."

"Thank you, Dear," Ethel said quickly, before Sarah could politely protest that she didn't intend for him to leave. "Now, Sarah, what is the matter? You look completely exhausted. Has something happened?"

"Oh, Ethel, I'm so upset. Peter Stewart came to see me yesterday." Sarah poured out the whole story. Ethel sat and listened while Sarah explained the proposal, the kiss, her reaction, everything.

When Sarah had finished, Ethel reached out and took her hand. "Oh, Sarah, I'm so sorry that this has happened. I feel so awful for teasing you about Mr. Stewart. But you did the right thing. You obviously cannot marry a man who isn't a Christian and who sees Christianity as a bargaining chip. I know you'll get over this experience and one day God will bring a fine Christian man into your life, just as he did for me. In fact, if you don't mind, I'd like to pray for just such a man for you."

"Thank you, Ethel," Sarah mumbled. "But just now I don't feel that I want to ever have anything to do with men again. And I have to go to Nairobi next week to pick up the supplies I ordered for the clinic. What if I run into Peter Stewart? I don't think I can face him. I don't think I can even be in the same town as he is, in case I run into him. I know I am overreacting, but I just don't know what I would say if I met him in the street."

"Listen, Sarah, I could use a trip to Nairobi to shop. Why don't I come with you? It would be fun to go together."

"Really? I'd be so grateful if you would, Ethel."

"Of course I would. We'll make it a pleasant day in

town, shopping and having lunch and getting all your work done too."

"Oh, Ethel, you're such a good friend. Thank you so much." Sarah went home that afternoon feeling much lighter in spirit.

❧

Kumani drove them down the dirt track in Sarah's lorry, bumping and bouncing all the way, with Sarah sitting in the middle next to him and Ethel by the door. It felt pleasant and companionable to be going together. Ethel had a few chores to do while Sarah made her report at the Mission House. Kumani would drive her, and then they planned to meet at the Lord Stanley Hotel at noon for lunch, as it was just around the corner from the Mission House.

"I only hope we don't run into Peter," Sarah said quietly to Ethel, not wanting Kumani to hear. Ethel reached over and squeezed her hand.

"Don't worry, my dear. Just hold your head high and say hello. You've done nothing to be ashamed of."

When Sarah walked into the cool darkness of the Mission House, blinking as her eyes adjusted after the brilliant midmorning sun outside, she found that Anita was still her old bubbly self. She was just bringing a tray of tea things out to the lounge.

"Oh, Sarah! How nice to see you. Come have tea with me. You're just in time for my tea break!" Sarah followed her into the lounge, and they sat down in the big overstuffed armchairs. "Well, how are you these days, Sarah? Your new clinic must be nearly finished now."

"It's coming along," Sarah replied, "and I'm doing well."

"Wonderful, you'll have to tell me all about it, but first I have something to tell you. The new doctor is finally here, and I want you to meet him! He's young and very nice. I think he's very handsome too. But he's just gone out for a moment. I hope he comes back soon, because I'm just dying to introduce you to him! You will make the perfect couple, a doctor and a nurse—"

"Wait a moment, Anita! You can't plan our marriage when we've never even met! Besides, it sounds to me as if you like him. Why don't you marry him?" Sarah laughed. Anita was always so enthusiastic, and the last thing she wanted just now were more complications in her life.

But Anita had already moved onto another subject. "Anyway, speaking of handsome, Sarah, have you heard from Peter Stewart lately?"

"No!" she lied, a little too vehemently. "But I really can't stay and chat, Anita. I came to Nairobi with Mrs. MacDougal, and she'll be back to fetch me at any moment, so I'd better fill in my report. I don't want to keep her waiting."

"Where is she?"

"At the market, shopping."

"Oh, for heaven's sake, Sarah, you have time for a chat. I haven't seen you for ages and ages. You are positively turning into a hermit these days. Besides, I want you to meet the new doctor, so you have to stay until he gets back!"

She sat down, and Sarah gave in and joined her on the couch. Anita gave her a smile and continued on. "So, you haven't heard from Peter? Then you'll not have heard that he is engaged!"

"Engaged?" Sarah said weakly. "To whom?"

"What's the matter? You look ill, Sarah. Are you alright?"

"Oh, yes, I'm fine." Sarah took one of the biscuits off the tray in front of her. "I must be a little hungry. I ate breakfast so early this morning."

"See, I told you, you should stay for a cup of tea. I'll pour you another cup and tell you all the latest." Anita picked up the teapot, not pausing to let Sarah get a word in. "You know, I was so hoping you would turn Peter Stewart into a Christian and then the two of you could get married. I still wish that had happened. He is so handsome and charming! I met him several times when I was at the hospital helping my father with the visiting. But I suppose it was not to be. Besides, I happen to know you'll meet a nice Christian man very soon!

"Anyway, as I was saying about Peter—Ruby Davis, you know, Jock's widow, helped Peter out quite a lot when he first came back to Nairobi."

The truth hit Sarah like stone before Anita told her. She was as shocked at her own reaction to Peter's engagement as she was to the news itself.

Anita rambled on, oblivious to Sarah's white face. "I suppose she must have been rather more helpful than we all thought because now they are engaged! Although, what with all the wild parties she throws and the fast crowd she associates with, I can't say I predict the marriage will last. Marriages with people like that never do, you know. I don't see anything good coming out of this marriage. But you never know, there was a couple I knew. . . ."

Sarah wasn't listening. She couldn't believe Peter

Stewart was actually marrying someone else. But of course, she should have known when she saw them together at the hospital. Ruby Davis was an attractive woman. If she wanted to sink her claws into Peter, well, he probably didn't have much hope of resistance. Or perhaps he didn't really want to resist. Well, it certainly was a good thing she had disposed of his proposal so quickly. He couldn't have been very deeply in love with her if he could rush off and propose to another woman within a month! She took another biscuit and bit into it savagely.

Peter Stewart really makes me angry! How could he have treated me that way, condescending to become a Christian, then offering me money to build a hospital if I married him? What a shallow, rude, unpleasant man he is!

"Reg, there you are!" Anita suddenly jumped up and ran to the door. Sarah looked up to see who had come in. A tall, dark-haired young man with very white skin entered the room. Anita was smiling an even more enthusiastic welcome than usual. The young man looked with interest at Sarah, but Anita was already clutching his arm and drawing him into the room. Of course, this must be the new doctor. Sarah smiled more warmly at the young man than she usually did when meeting people. Perhaps it was the news that she had just heard about Peter that made her glad to be meeting a Christian man.

"Sarah, I've been dying for you to meet our new young doctor, Reginald Bingley! Reg, this is Sarah Cameron. She has already started a nursing station out near Gilgil. Reg is spending a couple of months here in Nairobi learning Swahili before going out into the field. I just know you two will have so much in common!"

She turned back to Reg. "Sarah is so knowledgeable about everything to do with the African way of life, living as she does out there all alone among them! I don't know how she does it. It must be terribly lonely, but I admire her so much! Really, I do! Now, the two of you just sit down and get acquainted. I have work to do. I'll send out a fresh pot of tea!"

Reg reached out and shook her hand. "Miss Cameron, I'm so frightfully pleased to meet you at last. Anita has done nothing but talk of you since the day I arrived. She says you can tell me everything I need to know about the African and his medical difficulties. I would be so interested to learn from you!"

Sarah had taken his hand when he held it out, and now she tried to let go and sit down, but he held on to it and went on talking. "I am terribly excited to be here at last. I'm so anxious to begin my missionary work among the heathen. I have been praying and studying for so many years now, I can hardly believe I am here at last on the cusp of my calling!"

Sarah smiled again and finally pulled her hand away from the young man's grip. He certainly was enthusiastic about everything. Free at last, she sat back down on the couch. "I'm also just starting my work in Africa, so I'm not sure I can add very much to what you already know from medical school."

"Oh, but I do so want to come out to see your clinic. Anita tells me you have almost finished it. Of course, I won't be working with the Kikuyu people, but nevertheless, I'm sure the Wakamba tribe has similar medical issues. Would it be convenient for me to come out and see you this weekend? I could stay in Gilgil with the minister there, if it wouldn't be too much trouble."

"I'm sure it won't be any trouble at all. I am actually here in Nairobi with Ethel MacDougal, Ralph's wife. I'll bring her here to meet you on our way home this afternoon, and you can ask her yourself." Sarah put her teacup back down on the tray. "I'm afraid I cannot stay and chat much longer. Ethel will be along to fetch me any minute now. It has been a pleasure to meet you, Dr. Bingley, and I'll see you again this afternoon."

Reg jumped up and shook her hand again. "Oh, Miss Cameron, the pleasure has been mine, all mine! I have heard so terribly much about all you are doing, and I am honored to make your acquaintance at long last. I will look forward to seeing you and Mrs. MacDougal this afternoon. I can hardly contain myself at the opportunity of examining your clinic and all the work you are doing for our Lord among the heathen!"

Sarah had to forcefully pull her hand out from his again. But she couldn't fault him on his enthusiasm. "Good morning, Dr. Bingley," she said, following Anita out into the front parlor to the reception desk.

"There!" said Anita cheerily, as Sarah finished her paperwork "I told you, you needed a cup of tea and a bite to eat. The color is back in your cheeks, and you look ready to take on the world! You see, having a little chat with Reg has done you a world of good. I just knew the two of you would hit it off. You both have so much in common, and who knows what could come of it when you get to know each other a little more!" She winked at Sarah and laughed.

Sarah shook her head. "Anita, you are the most

romantically inclined person in the world. You never stop, do you?"

"Not when there is so much to be done! Besides, you have to admit you feel better now, don't you?"

"Alright, I admit it, but I'd better run, or I'll keep Ethel MacDougal waiting. Thank you very much for the tea and the chat, Anita. Bye!"

Sarah ran down the steps and rushed out onto the street. She was just hurrying up the garden path leading to the hotel entrance when she suddenly came face-to-face with none other than Peter Stewart himself. Ruby was hanging onto his arm, as she had been the last time Sarah had seen her.

"Sarah Cameron! How lovely to see you again. My, you are looking well."

"Thank you." Sarah stood rooted to the ground. Luckily, she was able to fall back on her nurse's training for something to say to him. "How are you feeling, Peter?" She looked into Peter's face. He looked rather tired and perhaps even a little strained.

"I'm very well, thank you, Sarah. I've been wondering how things are going with you. Is the clinic getting close to being finished yet?" He sounded nervous.

"Yes, it's coming along very nicely."

"Oh, that's good news, Sarah!" Ruby interrupted. "And have you heard our wonderful news?" Ruby turned to Peter. Sarah thought Peter's smile became rather wooden. "Peter and I are engaged! Do congratulate us!"

"Congratulations. I'm sure you'll both be very happy." Sarah was conscious that her smile was every bit as wooden as Peter's.

"Thank you! I knew you'd be glad to hear our news!"

She squeezed Peter's arm and beamed up into his face. Sarah thought she might be ill. Peter certainly didn't look terribly well either.

"Um, yes, well," Sarah was desperate to escape. "I'm afraid I can't chat, I'm in a bit of a rush. I'm meeting someone for lunch, and I'm already a few minutes late. I do wish you both well. Good-bye." She glanced quickly up at Peter before she turned away. His smile was still nailed firmly to his face. *I hope he feels good and guilty*, she thought, walking away as quickly as she could. It wasn't a kind thought, but she would deal with it when she got home. For now she simply had to concentrate on getting through the rest of the day without thinking about Peter Stewart marrying Ruby Davis.

The dining room in the Lord Stanley Hotel was cool, and a warm breeze blew in and ruffled the potted palms. The large open windows were shaded with shrubs and huge old trees. Yellow weaver birds flitted between their nests, which hung from the branches outside the window like little beehives. Crisp white linen tablecloths hung over tables covered with sparkling crystal glasses and gleaming silver cutlery. Waiters in long robes with colored cloth hats that reminded Sarah of upside-down flowerpots glided efficiently between the tables, serving the diners who spoke to each other in subdued voices.

"Is anything the matter, Sarah?" asked Ethel when they had placed their orders. "You seem rather distracted."

"I'm sorry, Ethel, I don't mean to be. I just bumped into Peter Stewart and Ruby Davis. They're engaged! Luckily Anita already told me about it this morning, so I wasn't caught completely off guard. But I can't believe it was only two weeks ago that he was proposing to me!"

Ethel looked puzzled for a moment. "My, that is rather sudden, isn't it? But perhaps you should think of it as good news, Sarah. After all, it means that you won't have to worry about him anymore. He will be someone else's husband."

"Yes, I suppose so. I was just a little overwhelmed by the news. Not only that, but when I bumped into Peter and Ruby, she was clinging to him like a limpet, begging me to congratulate them. I must say, at least Peter had the grace to look embarrassed."

"Why, Sarah Cameron, you almost sound as though you are jealous!" Ethel leaned back from the table, smiling gently at her new friend.

Sarah looked down. She spoke very quietly, "Yes, perhaps I am, Ethel. I really did like Peter. If he had been a Christian, I think I could have married him. I am just so confused by why God has let me go through all this. It would have been so much simpler if none of this had happened. It has not done anyone any good. Peter didn't become a Christian. Ruby lost her husband, and I am so mixed up by it all."

"Sarah, I don't know what God's plans in all this are either, but it is not the end of the story. He may have lessons that He wants you to learn from this. And you're wrong that not one good thing has happened. You did save Peter's life so that he still has a chance to become a Christian. You also told him about Jesus. Besides, you and I have become better friends through all this. God gives us Christian friends to help each other along the difficult paths we travel in life. We're not meant to be alone. We need to bear each other's burdens. Now we're friends, and that's a good thing."

"Thank you for being my friend, Ethel. God knew I really did need a friend. And you are right about the other things too. I'm just too upset at the moment to think of them for myself."

"I am only too glad to be your friend, Sarah. Remember, friendship is a two-way street. I needed a friend too."

"Ah, but you're married, and you have your husband to talk to."

"Yes, and my husband is my friend, but he doesn't replace other people in my life. I still need women friends who understand things from a woman's point of view. You'll know what I mean when you marry."

"If I marry, and that is a big if," Sarah commented dryly.

"You are a beautiful Christian woman, and I doubt you'll last long as a single person out here where women are so scarce. There are some fine Christian missionaries in need of wives. Perhaps I'll have to introduce you to some."

"No! Don't you dare! I have had enough of men to last me a lifetime. Besides, Anita is busy matchmaking for me already. She introduced me to Reg Bingley, the new doctor, this morning. Have you met him yet?"

"No, I haven't. Tell me about him. Is he nice? Is he handsome? Do you like him?"

Sarah had to laugh at Ethel. Her eyes were twinkling, and she was leaning forward, caught with a forkful of chicken halfway to her mouth.

"Yes, he's quite nice, and he's handsome too." Sarah paused. "He wants to come and stay with you so that he can come out and see my clinic. Anita has been telling him all about it."

"Of course he can stay with us! He sounds like just the thing you need to take your mind off Peter Stewart. You see, Sarah, where God closes a door, He opens a window. I can hardly wait to meet him."

"Ethel, it sounds as if you are the one who is looking for a husband, not me."

"Well, someone has to be excited about a new marriage prospect for you. I can't believe you haven't mentioned him to me until now. Sarah Cameron, you are an exasperating woman."

"Well, then let's see how you feel about this plan. We'll stop at the Mission House on the way home, and you can meet Dr. Bingley and invite him to stay with you. I told him this morning that I would ask you about his staying with you."

"That's a wonderful plan! Perhaps you are not as exasperating as I thought!"

The two women laughed, and Sarah described her whole meeting with Reg Bingley to Ethel, glad for a reason to forget about Peter Stewart and Ruby Davis for as long as she could.

After they had finished lunch, Kumani drove them over to the hospital, where Sarah's supplies were finally ready to be picked up. They spent the rest of the afternoon shopping, and at the end of the day, Kumani drove them over to the Mission House to meet Dr. Bingley.

When they walked into the lounge, Reg was already there. Sarah had the distinct impression that he had been waiting for her. And she found the warm, triumphant feeling this thought gave her quite pleasant. She especially appreciated the feeling after having run into Peter and Ruby. She set out to enjoy it to the fullest. Putting out her hand to shake Dr. Bingley's, she smiled very warmly up at him. He certainly was a tall, string bean of a man. But he was very nice. And a Christian too.

"Ethel, I'd like you to meet Dr. Reg Bingley. Dr. Bingley, Mrs. Ralph MacDougal."

"I'm so awfully pleased to meet you, Mrs. MacDougal. I have heard all about the tremendous work you and your husband do out here in the colonies, and I am just so pleased, as I said, to meet you. I do so look forward to meeting Rev. MacDougal too." Reg was shaking Ethel's hand the entire time he was speaking. He didn't stop even after he had finished.

"Ah, yes, Dr. Bingley. I am pleased to make your acquaintance also." She gently pulled her hand out of his, but this made poor Dr. Bingley even more uncomfortable. His hands suddenly darted in and out of his pockets and up to his head and back in and out of his pockets.

Sarah came to his rescue. "Yes, well, we must be heading off to Gilgil before it gets too late, Dr. Bingley, but I just wanted to introduce you to Ethel because she would be delighted to have you stay with her and Rev. MacDougal whenever you would like to come down to Gilgil."

"Oh, thank you, thank you so much, Mrs. MacDougal!" To the dismay of the two ladies, he reached over and took Ethel's hand and began shaking it again. "Would you mind terribly if I imposed upon you and your husband the week after next? I will have finished my Swahili course by the end of next week, and I do so want to see the country. I would like to come out and observe Miss Cameron's clinic, as I want to examine the native medical situation firsthand."

He stopped shaking Ethel's hand and turned to beam at Sarah. "Miss Cameron, would the week after next be convenient for you also? I don't want to impose upon you either, but I am terribly anxious to learn as much as I can about the situation here, and Anita tells me that you are so well informed. It would be an honor to watch you at work and learn from you. Even though I am a doctor and you are but a nurse, I am sure you have much to teach me."

Sarah smiled. She couldn't help comparing him unfavorably to Peter. He was awfully long-winded and perhaps even pompous, but his manners were immeasurably better. "Dr. Bingley, I would be delighted to have you come to my clinic. I hope you will find it interesting and informative. I'll look forward to seeing you!"

"And I, you, Miss Cameron, and I, you!"

"Good-bye, Dr. Bingley. I'll expect you at your earliest convenience a week from Monday."

"Thank you, Mrs. MacDougal, I will arrive on Monday. Of course, if that is convenient for your husband also. I would not want to impose on him. But then, I will be spending much of my time at Miss Cameron's clinic, so perhaps it won't be such an inconvenience for him."

"I'm sure that it will suit my husband very well, Dr. Bingley."

"Good-bye, Dr. Bingley," Sarah added. They turned and left the house. Kumani was waiting for them in the lorry.

As soon as they were seated and Kumani was weaving his way out of town between horses, carts, donkeys, and groups of women with bundles on their heads, Ethel turned to Sarah in the seat beside her. "Well! Dr. Bingley will certainly need some work if he is to become husband material. He's awfully nervous! And I wouldn't mind lopping off a few inches from his height so that we wouldn't have to crane our necks just to see his face. But there is one thing I can see for certain—he does admire you. He can hardly wait to come out and see you. And I'll warrant you there is more to attract him than simply your clinic."

"Oh, that's just because of Anita. Once he comes and gets to know me, he'll calm down considerably, I'm sure."

"I wouldn't be too sure. He's now spoken to you twice. And do you know, I think he was actually waiting for you at the Mission House when we arrived. I caught a glimpse of him watching us over the top of his newspaper as we arrived. Men don't behave like that just because they want to observe someone's place of work."

The warm, triumphant feeling crept into Sarah's heart again as Ethel spoke. It really was an improvement on the way she felt when Peter came into her mind. She could certainly enjoy living without the anger and the sudden surges of passion that had ravaged her composure lately. Yes, perhaps if Dr. Bingley still admired her when he visited next week, she would encourage him. She could already tell that Dr. Bingley was a man who held few surprises. He would behave with the utmost decorum and civility. Not like Peter.

eight

Once Sarah was home, work on the clinic progressed rapidly. She could hardly wait until it was finished. She expected to move in a week from Monday, the day Dr. Bingley was arriving. Perhaps this clinic would be the foundation for a real hospital here in the future, God willing.

Sarah noticed that she didn't think about Peter much during the day anymore, and she took it as a victory in her life. Only the evenings were still a bit difficult. Some nights on the veranda, when the wind blew through the bougainvillea the way it had the night Peter had kissed her, she felt herself aching for it to happen to her again. But, of course, not with Peter. She always remembered to add that to her thoughts. Peter had certainly complicated her life and opened up areas in her feelings that she had never given much attention to before.

Now and then she allowed herself to think of Dr. Bingley too. She found it surprising that he didn't come into her mind unbidden, the way Peter did. But perhaps it was just Dr. Bingley's natural politeness that made him less domineering even over her thoughts. She thought of kissing Dr. Bingley. If he still felt attracted to her, their relationship would eventually come to the point of physical touch. But she couldn't bring herself to imagine what the actual kiss would be like. Well, it didn't matter; if God had brought him into her life for marriage, God would give her the appropriate feelings. And they were sure to be different from the ones she had felt for Peter Stewart.

On the Sunday evening before Dr. Bingley would arrive, Sarah sat on the veranda reading her Bible. She came to the verse in the book of John, chapter ten, where Jesus said, "I am come that they might have life, and that they might have it more abundantly." The words seemed to speak to her aloud, even though she read them silently. Her skin prickled as she realized that it was Jesus' own voice she was hearing. For a minute she felt warm and intensely alive. He was saying to her that living life more abundantly was what she should be striving for. It was His goal for her life. "Abundant life" surely meant that she should open up her heart to the possibility of loving someone, even marrying him. Love between a husband and a wife was part of a full and abundant life. Avoiding love, even married love, if that was God's plan for her, would be wrong. As the sound of Jesus' voice faded away, she could still feel the shadow of elation and warmth lingering in her heart, like a whiff of perfume in the air when someone had just passed by.

She sat and listened to the wind rustling the papery bougainvillea petals, and she realized that up until now, she had not been living an abundant life. She had kept a part of her heart to herself, hidden away from anyone and protected from love. Peter had opened the part of her heart that she had always kept tightly locked. It was because she had known Peter that she could now choose to fall in love with Dr. Bingley, if that was God's plan.

God had therefore used Peter to show her how to begin to live more fully! Sarah felt so relieved that she could now understand why she had been through all the pain of knowing and loving Peter. She dropped onto her knees and thanked God.

In the morning, the day Dr. Bingley was to arrive in Gilgil, Sarah found it rather difficult to give her full attention to her patients. In the first place, she was exhausted. She had worked until late Saturday night moving everything into the clinic, and even on Sunday afternoon there was still work that had to be done. Now, on her first day in her new clinic, Sarah also found she had one eye on the window. She kept wondering if Dr. Bingley would arrive today or if he would stay with the MacDougals for the afternoon and walk up and see her in the morning. She felt almost certain he would come up right away.

When she saw his lanky figure approaching along the path with Kumani, midmorning, the newly familiar feeling of triumph swept quickly through her. She had been watching out for him, but she hadn't expected him to arrive this soon. He must have left Nairobi while it was still night! She couldn't help smiling to herself as she sent her patient out the door and washed her hands. Quickly, she whisked her brush through her hair. She was glad she had thought of bringing it with her this morning. She tried out a welcoming smile in the little hand mirror nailed above the basin and decided it would do. She walked out onto the veranda where her next patient was waiting and feigned a surprised look, which she quickly replaced with her welcoming smile.

"Dr. Bingley! I wasn't expecting you so soon! How nice to see you here already!"

"Oh, Miss Cameron, I am so thrilled to be here!" He strode up and took her hand and began shaking it vigorously. "I actually came to Gilgil last night. The MacDougals were kind enough to allow me to stay an extra night so that I could come out to see you this very morning. I am terribly excited to see all you are doing in service for the Lord."

He paused for a breath, and Sarah, feeling brave, clasped his hand with her free one so as to stop him shaking it. "Oh, Miss Cameron!" He turned pink and took his hand out of hers. "Oh, Miss Cameron! You look so well. I do hope I am not inconveniencing you by arriving so early. You still have patients to see. I won't be in your way, will I?"

"Of course not!" Sarah said warmly. But she knew he would. And she was right. He fussed and bothered his way behind her all the rest of the morning, and by the end of it, she had thoroughly had enough of him. But he certainly took her mind off Peter Stewart. She had too much else to think about, what with trying to listen to her patients and consider their treatments, while at the same time answering endless questions from Dr. Bingley.

"Please call me Reg," he said at one point in the morning.

"Then call me Sarah," she had responded, in the middle of securing a bandage over a large bite on the leg of a child who was squirming and crying in his mother's arms. She sent the boy off with his mother, giving her instructions to bring him back tomorrow so she could change the dressings. There were still patients to be seen, but Sarah stuck her head out into the waiting room and announced that she would return after lunch.

She walked up the shady path with Reg, wondering

what they would find to talk about as they sat eating lunch together. She needn't have worried.

"Sarah, thank you for being so informal with me. I didn't quite catch the reason that child, your last patient, was bitten so badly. My language studies have not made me used to the speed with which everyone speaks, you know. If these people would simply slow down to a more civilized pace instead of babbling on like Tennyson's brook, they would make themselves so much more clearly understood!"

Sarah turned to him, not sure whether to be irritated with his patronizing attitude or simply patient because he was new to foreign things. "Doc—er, Reg, I mean, you must realize that we sound as though we are babbling fast to them just as much as they do to us. We all speak quickly in a language that we are used to. For example, I found it difficult to catch everything when I was first learning Swahili, and now I can babble on just as quickly as they can. Just wait, you will too!"

"I am so glad I came to see you, Sarah. I'm so grateful to be on a first-name basis with you already. You have so much experience, and I am just sitting at your feet, catching pearls of wisdom, one after the other!"

Sarah laughed out loud at his extravagant metaphor, but stopped suddenly, realizing he was quite serious. She wondered if all Christian men were this serious and humorless. If they were, she thought wryly, she might have to revert to her original plan to remain single for the rest of her life.

They walked back to the clinic after lunch, and Reg dutifully followed her about all afternoon, endlessly questioning each diagnosis and decision she made. Finally, the long day drew to a close. Dr. Bingley thanked her profusely for all her patience with him as they walked slowly back up the path to Sarah's little house. She knew he was waiting to be invited in for supper, and he kept glancing hopefully up at the veranda, where Kumani had brought out a tray for supper. But Sarah really felt she couldn't sit and listen for one more minute to Dr. Bingley's praise of her patience and experience in the field. It had gone beyond flattering to simply tedious and extremely tiring. She was relieved when Kumani finally brought the lorry around to the veranda to pick up Reg and take him to the MacDougals'. She held out her hand. It was, after all, her first full day of work in her new clinic, and she was exhausted.

"I am so glad you were able to come so soon and spend the day with me, Reg. I would have loved to have had you stay for supper, but I confess I am utterly exhausted. I have been so busy all week moving into the clinic that I haven't really caught up with my rest. Perhaps you will be able to stay for supper another time? Please give my regards to Ethel and Ralph. Tell them I'll be down for a visit as soon as I can get away!"

She waved as Kumani drove off in a cloud of red dust, with Reg Bingley sitting rather sadly beside him.

But Sarah did not have a chance to visit Ethel again before a new and very unexpected development occurred. She sent Kumani to Gilgil to collect her mail one morning, and he returned with a letter for her from Peter Stewart. Sarah was flabbergasted. How could he possibly be writing to her after their furious fight, not to mention the fact that he had suddenly become engaged to someone whose own husband was barely cold in his grave!

Sarah stared at the letter, a little surprised at how strong her reaction to Peter still was. She thought she had achieved victory over her feelings for him. Suddenly, it crossed her mind that perhaps he had sent her an invitation to his wedding. She glared down at the envelope in her hand. It certainly did not look like an invitation. She decided she had better just get it over with and see what he wanted.

Dear Sarah,

I hope you can find it in your heart to forgive me for my unfortunate behavior when I visited you last month. I am truly sorry I caused you so much grief and embarrassment. I have been thinking deeply about how much you did for me when I was brought to you after the accident. You are a fine and truly kind lady, and I would be honored if you would still call me your friend.

As you know, Ruby and I will be getting married next year. She is anxious, however, to visit the site of Jock's death, just to put everything behind her before she begins a new life with me. She feels it will bring some sort of closure to her grief. I, too, would like to revisit the site, as I still feel responsible, at least in part, for the terrible accident. Perhaps it will help me to put my questions and fears to rest also.

We will be coming through Gilgil and traveling past your house next Wednesday, since the accident happened not far from there. Would it be alright if we stopped in for lunch? I would very much like to see you again and re-establish our friendship after

my ghastly mistake. Please forgive me.
  Let me know if we can come.

> *Yours very sincerely,*
> *Peter Stewart*

Sarah put the letter down and sank into the chair on the veranda where Peter had always sat. She felt as though she wanted to cry. Why couldn't he just go away and leave her alone? She didn't have enough time to think this through properly, and she couldn't talk to Ethel before she replied. She had to reply today, or the letter would never reach Nairobi before they left. He really was the most irritating man in the world. Why didn't he bother to write sooner? Perhaps she would just ignore the letter and say she hadn't received it in time.

No, she couldn't do that. Besides being an outright lie, he and Ruby might just come anyway. Perhaps the best thing to do would be to reply right away and tell him that she had not forgiven him for his behavior and did not want to be his friend.

No, that would go against her conscience. How could she call herself a Christian and yet refuse to forgive someone when he asked her to? Well, maybe she could say she forgave him, but didn't want to be his friend.

No, that was wrong too. What kind of witness would that be to non-Christians like Peter and Ruby? She would not be able to stand before God and ask for forgiveness for that one.

"Peter Stewart, you are the most annoying man in all of Africa!" Sarah said through gritted teeth. Then she picked up the letter and went inside to write a reply, telling him that he and Ruby were welcome to come, and if they wanted to stay with her, Ruby could sleep in the study/guest room, while Peter could have his usual spot on the veranda. Then she sent a letter to the MacDougals, inviting them for supper on Wednesday evening.

nine

Peter and Ruby arrived as planned on Wednesday morning. Sarah greeted them nervously, ignoring the butterflies that had suddenly sprung to life in her stomach. She was nervous and edgy, despite having spent the whole night in serious prayer about this visit. Ethel had replied to her invitation with an assurance that she and Ralph were praying for her too. It helped to know she was not alone.

As soon as their car came to a halt, Ruby jumped out and rushed over to Sarah and hugged her as though she were a long lost friend. Sarah immediately felt awkward and unfriendly, but she applied her best smile anyway and put out her hand to shake Peter's. Peter ignored it and kissed her on the cheek. As usual, Sarah's heart skipped. But she was surprised when she looked up at Peter afterward to see that he still didn't look very well. His face appeared drawn and worried and tired.

Ruby, on the other hand, looked wonderful. She was dressed in a red blouse and a narrow tan skirt. Her black hair was piled on top of her head—in an attempt to make her look taller, Sarah thought smugly.

Ruby bounced up the veranda steps and twirled around. "What a lovely little home you have here, Sarah! You've made it so cozy! And the view. It is magnificent. Why, you can practically see from one end of the Rift Valley to the other. How absolutely spectacular! Did you choose the site yourself? You certainly have an eye for location. All Peter told me about was the clinic you are so diligently building. He never mentioned a word about what a lovely spot you've chosen for it. Men! Aren't they just the most unpoetic creatures in the world?"

She flounced over to where Peter was now standing beside Sarah on the veranda and clamped onto his arm possessively. Peter immediately looked uncomfortable, or perhaps Sarah just imagined it.

"Well, you must be tired and dusty from your journey. Come inside and freshen up." Sarah was sure Peter relaxed a little as she whisked Ruby inside. When she came back out, Peter was sitting in his usual chair. Sarah sat in hers, and they looked out on the view together without speaking.

After a few minutes, Peter cleared his throat. "Thank you for letting us come and stay with you, Sarah. I'm so glad you've forgiven me. I really do value your friendship, and I am sorry I nearly ruined it. I was not myself at all when I returned to Nairobi. I thought I was well, but I wasn't. Not emotionally, anyway."

"Don't let's talk about it, Peter," Sarah replied quickly. "It's all water under the bridge now. Are you and Ruby planning to stay with me for a couple of days, as I suggested in my letter?"

"Yes, thank you so much for inviting us. I didn't like to ask, but Ruby isn't really keen on camping, you know. It would be so much more pleasant for her if we could stay with you. She really seems to admire you. Tomorrow we'll drive as far as the road goes, then walk in to the site where Jock and I were camping at the time, visit the site of the accident, and walk out. Then, if we could stay with you tomorrow night as well, we'll head back to Nairobi on Friday."

"Of course; that would be fine, Peter," said Sarah, turning her head as Ruby emerged from the house. Sarah thought she looked a little irritated. Perhaps she didn't like her talking so cozily to her fiancé. No, that was ridiculous. It was just her imagination playing the fool with her again. She got up and went in to tell Kumani they were ready for lunch.

When she came out, Ruby and Peter seemed to be sitting in an uncomfortable silence, but Ruby perked up when Sarah sat down. "Oh, Sarah, my dear, thank you so much for having us to stay. Peter has probably told you how much I dislike camping, with all the dust and the walking, and the inconveniences of it all. It is so much cozier just to stay here in your lovely little home."

Sarah smiled politely. "It's a pleasure to be able to help, Ruby."

Kumani brought out lunch, and they discussed the route Peter had planned for them the next day.

After lunch, Ruby said she would like to lie down and rest. Since they had made such an early start that morning, she was utterly exhausted. Peter said that he wanted to go out and look at how the clinic was progressing.

"It's almost finished," Sarah said excitedly. "I'll take you out and show you everything while Ruby has her rest. All the supplies for the examining room and the cupboards and the medicine to go in them are almost finished being moved in. I opened it to the Africans this very Monday. I am so thrilled to be doing the work God has called me to at last."

"I'm so glad I have seen the project grow almost from

the beginning. I practically feel as if it is mine too. I would love to have a look at the finished product and see how you've set everything up."

"You know, I think I'd like to see the clinic too," Ruby suddenly announced, forcing a rather hard smile. "I'll come with you."

"Oh, Ruby, you have been telling me all the way here how you hate getting up so early and losing all your beauty sleep! Just have a rest, and you'll feel much better! Sarah doesn't mind if you don't see the clinic right away. I'm sure there'll be other chances."

"No, of course I don't mind. Please let yourself rest, Ruby."

"No, I insist on seeing the clinic, Peter. I'm sure Sarah wouldn't mind showing it to me too." Ruby shot Peter a hard look, and he gave in.

Peter was interested in every detail of the clinic. He compared it to his father's practice in Aberdeen. Sarah was surprised at how much medical knowledge Peter had. It was a result of being the son of a doctor, she supposed. Ruby followed them around sullenly, only smiling when they addressed her directly.

"Come, let's go back to the house so you can rest a little before supper, Ruby," Sarah said at last.

They walked back down the path in the hot afternoon sun. The dust swirled in the arid wind. and the grass bristled dryly as they walked through it. It was definitely a hotter day than it had been lately. Sarah worried that the rains might be delayed. She had heard Kumani talking about it to the boy who came to look after her chickens and weed the garden. Peter and Ruby barely spoke to each other on the walk, and Ruby went to lie down as soon as they got back to the house.

Sarah was very glad she had invited Ethel and Ralph for dinner that night. She wanted Ethel to meet Peter. Also, she hoped the tension she had been feeling all afternoon between Ruby and Peter would be diffused with five of them at supper.

As the rest of the afternoon wore on, the atmosphere did not improve. Ruby rested for a little while, but insisted on coming out onto the veranda as soon as she heard Sarah and Peter talking. Sarah offered her tea and tried to make conversation with her and Peter, but it was an uphill struggle. They had so little in common. Ruby wasn't particularly interested in Sarah's work, and Sarah didn't know any of the people Ruby knew in Nairobi. And neither did she have any idea what the latest fashions were in London, nor had she been to a single horse race at the racetrack where the Nairobi social set liked to go to see and be seen. Peter tried to talk of the plans Sarah had for the clinic, but Ruby changed the subject.

"You are so selfless, Sarah, giving your life to improving the lot of the natives, but I don't believe we should really spend so much time and money worrying about them. They have managed to survive for eons the way they are. If they had wanted a better life, they would have worked for it. They are perfectly happy the way they are, and we should leave them alone. Besides, we let them work for us and earn what money they need. And anyway, I don't believe they have the capacity to truly appreciate culture and civilization."

But Sarah had heard these ideas before, and she was prepared to argue. "The Africans love their children and their families as much as we do. They want them to be healthy and live long, productive lives. I don't believe anyone should have to live without proper medical care if it is available to them. Not only that, Jesus has commanded us to go and make disciples of all the nations. The African has as much right to hear the gospel as we do." Sarah felt herself getting a little heated as she spoke. She hated the smug attitude some of the settlers had toward the native population.

Peter must have sensed her anger building because he suddenly interrupted to change the subject again. "Ruby, did I ever mention to you that Sarah took her nurse's training under my father in Aberdeen? We discovered we actually have several acquaintances in common back in Scotland. You know, Sarah, I am planning to take Ruby to Scotland on our honeymoon to meet my parents."

"Yes, he is," Ruby chimed in, easily distracted by honeymoon plans. "But I am not fond of cold weather, and it will be the middle of winter when we are there. We will, of course, spend most of our time in London, where we can go shopping and have wonderful parties and meet interesting people. And the weather in London is far more bearable. I can't abide cold, miserable weather!"

Sarah looked at her watch. She was getting thoroughly tired of trying to converse with Ruby. It wouldn't be much longer before the MacDougals' car would come winding up the hillside. It also occurred to Sarah that Ruby probably enjoyed a "sundowner" drink at this time of the day, as it was the social custom among the settlers. She could at least offer her a cool beverage. "Would you like a glass of lemonade, Ruby?"

"You don't have anything a little stronger, do you,

Sarah? I could really do with a gin and tonic about now."

"No, I'm awfully sorry, but I don't drink, and I don't keep liquor on hand either. I rarely have visitors who drink liquor."

"We'll both have some lemonade, Sarah," Peter quickly announced, at the same time shooting a warning glance at Ruby before she said anything else.

Sarah was immensely relieved to hear the loud roar of the MacDougals' motorbike and sidecar coming up the hill. She jumped up and ran down the veranda steps to meet them.

Meanwhile, Ruby, who must have assumed that Sarah was out of earshot, or perhaps not caring if she wasn't, leaned over and hissed to Peter, "My word, first I can't even get a drink at the end of a long, hard day, and now we have to spend the whole evening with a minister! This was an absolutely frightful idea of yours to stay here!"

"Oh, shut up, Ruby!" Peter hissed back between clenched teeth.

"Hello, Ralph," Sarah said a little too cheerily as the MacDougals emerged stiffly from the motorbike. She leaned forward to hug her friend Ethel. "The visit is a ghastly ordeal!" she muttered in Ethel's ear.

"Why, Sarah, I'm thrilled to meet your friends at last," Ethel said brightly, letting Sarah go and marching up the steps of the veranda. "I've heard so many wonderful things about you, Peter! And this must be your fiancée."

Sarah made the introductions and explained that they would be having dinner a little earlier than usual because the MacDougals had a long drive home and Peter and Ruby were starting out early in the morning. She then went inside and explained this change of plans to Kumani and the cook, begging them to get supper out to the veranda as quickly as possible.

Supper was difficult and strained. Ruby was clearly in a bad mood, and she made no effort to talk to the MacDougals. No one seemed to know what questions to ask. Peter described how well he had recovered from the accident, but it was awkward to talk of Jock with Ruby there and engaged to Peter. Afterward, as they were sitting on the veranda sipping coffee in the cool evening air, the atmosphere between the five of them at last relaxed slightly. Ralph asked Peter if he was worried about being gored by a rhino again when he resumed his safaris.

"I am not so worried about dying myself, anymore," Peter replied with a rueful chuckle. "But I do have nightmares about a client being killed again."

"Yes, it was a terrible tragedy, wasn't it? I hear that it was the fault of a gun bearer shooting a rifle and startling the rhino. There are some things only God can control," Ralph replied. Sarah held her breath, interested to see what Peter would think of that.

"Actually," Peter leaned forward in his chair, as if he were making an important point, "I am beginning to believe it was God who saved my life. I was a hairsbreadth from bleeding to death, and if I had been anywhere else when the rhino charged, I would certainly have died. The last thing I remember doing as the rhino charged was praying." He chuckled suddenly. "If you call shouting 'God, please help me!' praying. Then, I don't know if I was dreaming or not, the next thing I remember was waking up in the night, and I heard Sarah praying, 'God, help him. Please help him.' It made a clear impression on me. I concentrated on getting well as quickly as I could after that."

"Humph," Ruby snorted, "Everybody prays when they are about to die. It is an instinctive response. It doesn't mean anything."

Ralph responded quickly, "I don't agree with that, Ruby. I believe that people deep down inside realize that there is something or someone bigger and more powerful than they are. When they are in a life-and-death situation, it concentrates their mind and the extraneous distractions of life are erased for a moment, and they cry out to God to help them.

"We should realize that we are actually in a life-and-death situation every day of our lives. One day we will all die, and we need to think about that fact now, before it is too late. Peter is fortunate because he has been taken to the brink and then returned. Now, he truly understands how fragile life is. And he thinks about God differently. Don't you, Peter?"

"Well, I suppose I have some questions about God that I didn't have before, but I'm not sure I have actually come to any conclusions about Him."

"I certainly have," Ruby announced. "If He cared about me, He would have let Jock live too, not just Peter. Why should He care more about Peter than Jock? That is not fair of Him, is it?"

"Maybe Jock didn't pray," Peter said.

"How do you know he didn't pray? You did, so why couldn't he have prayed too?" Ruby's voice was shrill and harsh.

"No one knows the mind of God, Ruby," Ralph said, trying to diffuse her anger. "None of us but God Himself knows if Jock prayed, or even why He took one man and left the other."

"Whenever you Christians come to a difficult question, you always say something like that: 'No one knows what God thinks,' or 'God moves in mysterious ways,' or 'It was God's will.' I think you are just too frightened to face the truth that God does not exist."

Peter answered her this time. "I've given it a lot of thought since the accident, and I think you are wrong. I know I was being watched and cared for by a higher power. I really felt it. Obviously, I can't answer for Jock, but as for me, I've begun to wonder if there isn't something to the Christian faith, after all. I know I didn't recover from my injuries alone."

"Well, I think you are still a little affected by the terrible ordeal you've been through, Peter. I hope you get over it soon. Anyway, I am very tired, so if you will all excuse me, I think I'll go to bed." Ruby got up.

Ethel jumped up as well. "Yes, we must go too. Come along, Ralph, let's be on our way. We have a long drive."

Ralph stood up and held out a hand to Peter. "It has been a pleasure to meet you at last, Peter. If you ever feel you want to discuss Christianity, please come and see me. I do love a good chat about religion. Especially when the person is posing interesting questions, as you are."

"Thank you. I might just take you up on that offer," replied Peter, shaking his hand.

Sarah walked them down the path to their bike. She said good-bye quickly and thanked Ethel for praying for her. Ethel replied that she could see Sarah needed it. They got on the bike and drove into the night.

Sarah could hear angry voices on the veranda as she walked back to the house. Ruby was shrieking, "How dare you go around telling people you prayed and that is why God saved you and not Jock? How unbelievably arrogant can you possibly be? Ever since we've arrived, you've been trying to impress Sarah with your holier-than-thou attitude! 'Ruby and I will just have a glass of lemonade, Sarah.' And, 'Sarah, tell me all about your wonderful clinic for the natives. The natives will be so grateful for all you are doing, Sarah!' "

"Ruby! Keep your voice down. You are behaving like a fool. Just go to bed."

"Hah! Bed! 'Ruby, you'll be sleeping in the study, and Peter will be out on the veranda.' What is she going to do, post a guard to make sure we don't get up to any hanky-panky in the middle of the night?"

Sarah had stopped at the bottom of the steps. She was staring up at the scene, openmouthed, not knowing whether to just run away or walk up and pretend she hadn't heard anything at all. But at that moment, Ruby turned and glared at her, then marched into the house. The door to the study slammed.

Sarah looked at Peter, who spoke quickly. "I'm so sorry, Sarah. She must be upset about going out to the accident site. That's the only reason I can think of for her behavior. I've never seen her this angry before. I'm sure she'll have recovered her good sense by morning."

"Yes, you are right; she must be upset about tomorrow." Sarah walked past him and paused at the door to the house. "You know the routine here, so I'll just go to bed. Good night, Peter."

"Good night."

Sarah went into her room and lay on the bed without bothering to undress. She was breathing hard, as if she had been running, and her heart was beating loudly. She went over and over Ruby's words in her mind. She decided that it wasn't the words themselves that were so unkind, as the simpering, whiny voice she used to imitate Peter, mocking him directly to his face. As for her prissy imitation of Sarah's voice—"And you'll be sleeping on the veranda, Peter"—Sarah could hardly think of it without wanting to get up and slap Ruby's face. The more she replayed the scene in her mind, the angrier she became, until she finally jumped up off her bed and began pacing back and forth in the darkened room, muttering sharp retorts under her breath that would put Ruby in her place once and for all.

At last she threw herself back down on her bed. She began to think of Peter. What was he doing, taking up with a woman like that? Obviously Sarah didn't know him very well at all because she had actually been tempted to accept his proposal of marriage. Anyone who would see both Ruby Davis and herself as potential wives obviously had some serious problems judging character.

Aloud, she prayed, "Thank you, Lord, for helping me to resist the temptation of marrying Peter Stewart. And thank You for bringing him and Ruby here, so that I can see him for what he really is and put him out of my heart and my mind forever. I was afraid to see him again, Lord, but now I see why You brought him here. Thank You from the bottom of my heart."

Sarah lay quietly for a few moments. She wondered what the time was. It must be very late. No doubt Peter and Ruby would be getting up in a few hours to head off into the bush. She should really get up and see them off.

It would be polite. She decided she would just doze in her clothes so she wouldn't have to bother dressing again in an hour or two. She pulled the covers over her, but she didn't fall asleep for a long time. When she finally dropped off, it was only to be awoken a few minutes later by a soft knock on the door. Peter was standing in the gray morning light.

"Sorry to wake you, Sarah. We're on our way. Ruby is still in a bad mood, so we won't be coming back to stay with you this evening. We'll just go right on through to Nairobi. But I wanted to say good-bye to you and tell you how sorry I am for what happened last night."

"Don't mention it, Peter. I'm sure it will all turn out well in the end. I wish you and Ruby all the happiness in the world, and may God bless you both." Sarah put out her hand to shake Peter's, pleased with her magnanimous speech.

But again, Peter leaned forward and kissed her cheek. Then he wrapped her in his arms and held her for a few moments. Sarah didn't resist. It just felt so good to feel his arms around her that she didn't have the strength to pull away from his embrace.

"Good-bye, Sarah. I think of you often." He drew back and looked down into her face. She did not trust herself to say anything. "Remember me now and then, will you?"

She said nothing. She wanted so badly to say something warm yet flippant, kind yet humorous, but all she could do was look up into his soft blue eyes and lose herself in them.

Without a word, he turned and left, disappearing into the grayness of the cold morning light.

Sarah dredged a long sobbing sigh from the very

bottom of her heart. Why, oh, why did he always touch her so deeply?

Slowly, she turned and went back to bed. She could hear the car driving down the road. "Well, the worst is over," she sighed and fell deeply asleep.

ten

Sarah hoped the shock on her face would disguise the sudden surge of joy that electrified her body when Ethel told her the news as they sat having tea on Ethel's veranda one afternoon: Peter Stewart had broken his engagement to Ruby Davis.

She simply could not control the way she felt about this man, and the last two weeks had been a long, grim testament to the fact. Despite the brilliant sunshine in which Sarah spent her days, the hard work she put into making the clinic everything she had dreamed of, and the pleasure she derived from working with sick people and helping them back to health whenever she could, she could not erase the dark hopelessness of her mood underneath it all. It was more frustrating than she ever imagined. Nothing touched her heart. She could not scrub away the stain of hopelessness no matter how hard she worked. No matter how hard she prayed either. And now, at the mere mention of this new situation, her heart jumped with joy. All she could do was hope the shock covered her feelings.

"It must make you so pleased, hearing this news, Sarah, after all you've done for him," Ethel said, sipping her tea.

Sarah stared at her in horror. So Ethel knew that she was still struggling with her feelings for Peter. They must be written all over her face, then!

"Yes," Ethel continued, "I know it must have been so frustrating to have saved the man's life, only to have him throw it away again on loose living and loose women. Ralph says Peter is coming very close to making a Christian commitment too."

Sarah let out a huge sigh of relief. She had only been reading her own feelings into Ethel's perfectly innocent words. "I am so glad to hear that news, Ethel," she answered quickly. "I was very upset when Peter became engaged to Ruby Davis. She really did try to prevent Peter from taking any interest at all in the Christian faith. I heard her say so, myself. It just goes to show how powerful prayer really is, doesn't it? I think it is the prayers we all offered for Peter's salvation, both physical and spiritual, that have prevented him from going down the wrong path and marrying Ruby."

"It certainly must be prayer that has brought about this tremendous change in his life. And Ralph says Peter has become so interested in every aspect of the Christian faith and has actually been to church in Nairobi twice. He came and spent the day with Ralph a week ago. He said he was on his way to spend some time with someone he knows in Uganda. But he is going to stop in and have another visit with us on his way back to Nairobi. When he does I'll arrange to bring him up here to visit with you. He asks about you all the time, you know."

"Oh, no!" Sarah exclaimed. Ethel looked at her in surprise. "I mean, it isn't that I don't want you to bring him, it is just that, well, I am so busy with my clinic now, and I won't have time to spend with him." Sarah knew as she spoke the words that this was a silly thing to say.

There was silence for a moment. Ethel stared at her.

"Sarah?" She spoke slowly and carefully. "You are still in love with him, aren't you?"

Sarah sat quietly. She let her silence be her answer.

"Sarah, don't judge yourself too harshly for it. You are a woman, and sometimes you just fall under the influence of a nice man, that's all. Tell me, have you heard from Reg Bingley lately? Do you think you could feel the same way about Reg as you do about Peter?"

Sarah rolled her eyes heavenward. "I honestly don't know if I can ever feel about anyone the way I feel about Peter. But Reg is certainly trying hard to make me fall in love with him. There has hardly been a day go by when I haven't heard from him."

"Really!" Ethel's eyes lit up with anticipation at a happier romance in Sarah's life. "How exciting! I knew he was interested in you. He couldn't stop talking about you all the time he was at our house. He is a very nice young man. Don't tell me you are not interested in him, Sarah. A nice Christian doctor would make a wonderful husband for you."

"Hold your horses, Ethel MacDougal. I've laid eyes on the man exactly twice. I'm not ready to accept a proposal of marriage yet, my dear!"

Ethel laughed, but she had a knowing look in her eye. "Don't tell me you haven't thought about the possibility, Sarah. You are, after all, a woman, and you can't be completely unaware of Dr. Bingley's intentions toward you!"

Blushing, Sarah had to admit that the thought of marrying Dr. Bingley had crossed her mind. "But he is so serious, Ethel. He takes everything so literally and so humorlessly. I am afraid I would find myself slipping in the odd sly comment or sarcastic word here and there. I don't know if I can control my tongue. Do you find Ralph terribly serious all the time like Dr. Bingley?"

"I'm afraid Ralph is the one who finds me serious! He is always teasing me about the things I go on about. For instance, just this morning he was teasing me about how I was getting dressed up as though I was about to go to tea with Queen Victoria instead of going to a missionary clinic in the dark heart of Africa."

Ethel rambled on for a long time about the way Ralph teased her all the time. Sarah could see their marriage was happy. Ethel's eyes sparkled, and her face was animated and joyful when she talked about her husband. Sarah tried to imagine herself talking like that about Reg Bingley. She couldn't.

But Peter, well, that was another matter. And there he was again, slipping slyly into her thoughts when she least needed him there. Reg Bingley was supposed to be in her thoughts. At least she could rest assured now that Peter was not in danger of throwing his life away in an unfortunate marriage.

As she ate supper on the veranda that evening, she thought over the new development in Peter's life. She secretly wondered if the broken engagement had anything to do with the argument he and Ruby had had when they visited her. She didn't think so. If Peter had been serious about his faith, then he would not have become engaged to Ruby in the first place. Probably the reason he had become serious about his faith was because of the breakup and not that his faith actually led to the breakup. In that case it would be another one of God's plans to bring something good out of something bad. And that was also a reason for thankfulness.

She had to go to Nairobi next week. For the last two weeks she had been trying not to think about it. There was a conference coming up for all the missionaries in the country to report on their work and progress in the field, and Sarah had been dreading it. In the first place, she knew that she would be seeing Reg Bingley. He had mentioned several times in recent letters how much he was looking forward to seeing her at the conference.

She didn't know what to do about him. Ethel was right, a Christian doctor would make a tremendous husband. But she wasn't sure she could fall in love with Reg Bingley, the man. And she was sure the minute she arrived at the conference he would want to be with her. What should she do? She didn't want to write Reg Bingley off. He was a good Christian man, after all. Perhaps she should try to be less critical of him.

But Reg Bingley was not the real reason she was worried about going to the conference in Nairobi. She was afraid she would run into Peter. Nairobi was not large, and she would be there for a whole week. She knew she really had no particular reason to give another thought to Peter Stewart, yet the prospect of accidentally meeting him kept him in her thoughts. On the other hand, Reg Bingley could very well be the man God intended for her, and she should try to think about developing a relationship with him when she went to Nairobi.

❧

The Mission House was abuzz with activity when Sarah arrived the following Sunday evening. Missionaries were arriving and suitcases were being unloaded from cars and carriages. There were hugs and hellos everywhere she turned. The normally quiet house was bustling with people coming in and out.

Kumani had barely taken Sarah's suitcase out of the car when she heard a familiar voice. "Miss Cameron! Sarah! Hello, I've been waiting for you all afternoon!"

Sarah knew Reg would have been waiting, so she had delayed her arrival until just before dinner. She gave him her best warm smile and felt like a hypocrite. Smiling at Peter was so easy compared to this. But perhaps she just needed to get used to Reg before she felt comfortable with him.

"Yes, I had so much to do before I left home," she said. "But it is wonderful to be here at last!" She turned to the desk, where Anita was telling everyone what their sleeping arrangements were.

After she had checked in, Reg offered to show her to her room. She noticed Ralph MacDougal in the lounge talking to a group of missionaries. He waved cheerfully, but Reg was leading her down the hallway. He carried her suitcase up the stairs and deposited it in her room for her. "I'll see you at supper," he said. "It's in half an hour."

Sarah found that she was staying in a room with three other single women, all of whom were much older than she was and who knew each other very well. Florence Wood was one of the organizers, so she would rarely be in the room. Mabel MacRae and Jane Harrison, the other two women, were already dressing for dinner, but they turned and greeted her kindly.

"It warms my heart to see young women going into the mission field, my dear," said Miss MacRae. "The young people of today seem only interested in having parties and getting married. It is not the way it was when I was young. The young people of my day were much more serious about the Christian faith. It is not like that with the modern youth, I dare say!"

"Quite so, my dear Mabel," agreed Miss Harrison.

"Is dinner at seven o'clock?" asked Sarah, changing the subject.

"Seven o'clock sharp, Florence says," Miss MacRae announced importantly. "We have a lot of business to attend to after dinner, so she wants everyone to keep to a strict schedule. Florence is not one to dillydally about the place, wasting time!"

"Yes, Miss MacRae, I'm sure she isn't," Sarah replied, pouring some water into the basin at the washstand to clean off the grime of her long trip. She could already see that the less time she spent in her room, the better. Reg Bingley would be pleased about that, she thought wryly.

Reg was waiting at the dining-room door for Sarah when she came down for supper. He had managed to be seated next to her at one of the three long tables. Sarah was relieved to find that Anita was sitting on her other side. Miss MacRae and Miss Harrison were at another table with some of the older, long-standing missionaries in the area. Rev. Featherington, who was also sitting at that table, stood and welcomed them all to the conference. He said grace, and in minutes, bowls of steaming tomato soup were brought in. The noise of chatting suddenly died away while the hungry diners attended to their suppers.

"Frightfully good soup, isn't it?" commented Reg to Sarah.

She was just turning to agree with him when Anita leaned over and whispered in her ear. "Have you heard the latest news about Peter Stewart?" And without waiting for her answer, she added, "Ruby Davis and he are no longer engaged! It is quite the scandal!"

"Yes, it is delicious!" said Sarah to Reg.

"What! You know about it!" Anita gasped.

"No, I meant the soup."

"Know about what?" inquired Reg.

"Peter Stewart and Ruby Davis," whispered Anita dramatically.

"Yes, I have already heard that they broke off their engagement," said Sarah firmly, and changing the subject, she turned to Reg and said, "How is your Swahili coming, Reg? Have you had much chance to practice since we last spoke?"

"Oh, but I have!" said Reg, obviously delighted to be asked. "Why, the very day after you so kindly had me helping at your clinic, I was able to go out on a trip to a village near Lake Navasha and we. . ."

Anita leaned over and whispered in Sarah's ear. "There's more to it than that. It is the talk of the town! You must let me tell you as soon as you can get away!"

"And then, just yesterday," Reg was continuing, "I spent the day at the native hospital here in Nairobi, working with Dr. Daniels. He was most impressed with how quickly I have picked up the language."

Luckily, Reg didn't expect much from Sarah but to nod and smile. Her mind was back at home, going over everything she had heard Ruby telling Peter the night they had their huge argument. What on earth had happened to them that she didn't know about? How soon could she get away to talk to Anita?

Sarah turned to Reg. "What will you be doing now that your language training has finished? Do you have an assignment to a mission station yet?"

"I have had several meetings with Rev. Featherington about my assignment. It is rather up in the air at the moment, as there is a certain item of information I must ascertain before I can make a decision about my future. I am hoping to be able to discover the missing information here this week, Sarah."

Sarah was surprised to see Reg turn a warm shade of red and look down at his lap and adjust his napkin several times. Then he glanced up into her face, and suddenly Sarah knew exactly what he meant by the missing information. It drove Peter and Ruby completely out of her mind altogether. She looked away from Reg, down into her lap also.

Anita, who hadn't missed a single piece of this little charade, was positively bubbling with suppressed enthusiasm. Sarah felt her nudge her, and she saw her smile excitedly at Reg. "Oh, Dr. Bingley, I do hope you will tell me as soon as you know this information. I love to be let in on secrets!"

"Never fear, Miss Webster, I will let you know the minute I am made aware of the news myself." He smiled down at Sarah, who was now fiddling intensely with her own napkin. She heard them both laugh knowingly over her head.

She could not decide what her feelings for Dr. Reg Bingley were, no matter how much she twisted her napkin. Someone took away her soup plate and replaced it with a dish of fish. But she did have to admit there was something thrilling and flattering about being the subject of a romance. She just wished she could erase the annoying sense that she was not actually in love with Reg

Bingley. After all, he was the perfect husband for her. He was a doctor and a missionary, and most importantly of all, he appeared to be very much in love with her.

There must be something very wrong with her. She could fall like a stone for someone as inappropriate as Peter Stewart in a heartbeat, yet a good, solid Christian man like Reg Bingley was not good enough for her.

Reg was eating his fish. Sarah glanced covertly over at him. He wasn't even a bad-looking man either, in a long, thin sort of fashion. She decided that she must simply swallow her feelings of doubt about Reg, and if he did propose to her, she would accept. After all, how many other chances would she have at such a good marriage? None, she was very sure.

She smiled warmly at Reg. "You will tell me as soon as you know too, won't you?" she teased.

A glowing smile spread across Reg Bingley's face. "Sarah, you will be the first to know!"

Sarah blushed again. She was enjoying this, even though that nagging doubt was still flitting through the back of her mind. Never mind, she would get rid of it in time.

Dinner was long and delicious. Sarah, Anita, and Reg chatted happily about the joys and frustrations of living in Africa, of how they all missed family back in England and Scotland, and of all their mutual acquaintances. Anita also filled Reg in on all the details about the people he hadn't met yet.

"Please, Miss Webster, call me Reg. I don't stand on formality, you know. Sarah has already graciously agreed to be on a first-name basis with me. You would do me an honor if you would too."

"Why, of course, Reg," Anita replied easily. "And you must call me Anita. Sarah does, you know."

They all laughed. Sarah wished she could be as at ease with Reg Bingley as Anita seemed to be. But then, Anita didn't have to decide whether to accept his proposal and be joined in holy matrimony to the man forever.

Anita and Reg chatted on happily, but again and again, Sarah found her thoughts wandering to what it was that she had not heard about Peter and Ruby.

When supper and the meeting that followed were at last over, Sarah could see that Reg wanted her to stay downstairs in the parlor and chat with him for a little while. But she explained how tired she was from her long day and that she must really turn in. "Besides," she said conspiratorially, "Miss MacRae and Miss Harrison will be watching me closely to see that I do not engage in any improper modern behavior that the youth of today are so prone to."

She was just about to laugh at her own joke, when Reg responded, "Yes, they are quite right. You must not behave improperly. You would be the only young lady left in the parlor if you stayed. They are quite right. Good night, Sarah. I do hope you have a very restful night, and I look forward to seeing you in the morning!"

"Good night, Reg," Sarah replied with a sigh and turned to go upstairs.

She wondered if she could find Anita anywhere. She had disappeared to correct a mistake in someone's registration papers that had been brought to her attention after the meeting, and Sarah hadn't seen her since. She didn't think she could sleep if she didn't find out what was happening to Peter and Ruby that had everyone in town talking. She headed up the stairs to find Anita.

I'll just hear about it, and it will be one of Anita's gossipy exaggerations. Then I can put it to rest and get a good night's sleep.

But Anita was obviously as excited about telling Sarah the news as Sarah was to hear it. She was waiting for Sarah on the landing. "I thought Reg would have persuaded you to stay and talk with him in the parlor," she whispered, as Sarah reached her.

"No, he didn't want me to behave improperly in front of the Misses MacRae and Harrison," said Sarah.

"Oh, really?" Anita replied curiously, but Sarah didn't explain.

"Anita, tell me what happened to Peter and Ruby that has caused such a scandal. I've already heard they are no longer engaged."

"Yes, that is why I was waiting for you. Come, let's go out onto the balcony."

"I'll just go into my room and fetch my shawl. I can tell the misses that I am just having a quick chat with you. I saw them glaring at me as I spoke to Reg when he carried my bags up to my room, and I don't want them to think I stayed to talk with him!"

The balcony was cool and fresh after the stuffy dining room. Sarah loved the night sounds of Africa, the insects, the frogs, and the birds that sang in the evening. She could smell the African fires smoking somewhere in the distance, and now and then a car rattled past on the road beyond the oleander hedge. She and Anita leaned over the railing. It was just a small balcony, and there were no chairs. The damp, earthy smell of the garden, mingled with sweet perfume of flowers Sarah didn't know the names of yet, rose to envelope them. For a fleeting moment Sarah thought about Reg. An African night might add just the romantic touch she needed to fall in love with Reg. Perhaps those lovely evenings in the darkness of her veranda were the reason she had fallen in love with Peter.

"So you've heard that Ruby broke off her engagement to Peter then?" Anita was saying.

"Yes, but I thought it was he who broke it off."

"Oh no! Where did you hear that? It was most certainly her doing. I'm sure of it. She is the one who says it is his fault that her husband was killed. That is why she broke it off. She says she found out things about Jock's accident that she didn't know before."

Sarah was confused. "I think you had better start at the beginning, Anita. I don't understand what you mean. She found out things about Jock's accident? What things? How?"

Anita was ready. "Well, she and Peter went out to visit the site of the accident. But, of course, you know that because they were staying with you."

"Yes, but they never went out there. They had an argument, and she told Peter that she wanted him to take her back to Nairobi."

"Well, they must have gone after all because she says she went to the site, and when they were there, Peter broke down and confessed to her what had really happened."

"What happened?"

"It seems that Peter had been told by his African guides that there were rhino in the area, but he wanted to get one so badly before he left that he wasn't as careful as he should have been. He took a bad shot at a rhino and missed. The shot frightened the rhino, and then it charged Jock, who was the closest person to it.

"Peter should have made sure that Jock was not in the vicinity before he shot. But he was not close enough to get off a good shot and kill the rhino before it reached Jock. Ruby says Peter then tried to get the rhino to charge him too so that he could claim he tried to save Jock's life, but the rhino was eventually scared off by the African guides firing into the air, not by Peter. It just gave him a glancing blow with his horn.

"Ruby is also telling everyone that when Peter stayed with you for such a long time, it was only to hide the fact that his injuries were not as severe as they should have been if he had really tried to save Jock's life!"

Sarah was stunned. For a second she panicked and wondered if Ruby could be right and she had actually been lied to by Peter. But she remembered his wounds. They were definitely not caused by a mere "glancing blow."

Anita continued. "Anyway, Ruby is spreading the rumors that no one can find Juma, the gun bearer, because Peter paid him off to get lost so that the real story wouldn't come out. And she is telling people that anyone who goes on one of Peter Stewart's safaris is risking his life. I think she is setting out to ruin his reputation and his business. And it looks as if she is succeeding. I don't know if Peter will ever be able to find clients in this town again."

Sarah stared at Anita, openmouthed. Could Peter have really lied to her too? Everything she knew about what happened in the rhino accident came from what Peter himself had told her. She stammered her question aloud. "But, Anita, Peter should have been killed by the rhino. If he had arrived at my clinic even a few minutes later, he would have been dead. It was not a glancing blow the rhino gave him."

Anita shrugged. "I really don't know, Sarah. I'm just telling you what Ruby is saying about the whole thing."

"I can't believe Ruby's story, Anita. Peter is not a liar. He wouldn't lie to me like that." Sarah wished her own words were as convincing as she tried to make them sound.

But Anita shook her head. "I can't speak for Peter. I hardly know the man."

"Well, what is Peter doing about it? Has anyone heard his side of the story?"

"That's another bad thing. He is not saying anything at all. In fact, no one seems to know where he is. He left town a week or so ago. People say he was last seen in your part of the country, but no one seems to know for sure. It doesn't make him look very good, does it?"

Sarah's mind was racing. He left a week ago? Wasn't that when he had been to visit Ralph and Ethel? Had he lied about his interest in their faith? Was he just making an excuse to visit them because he was trying to hide from the truth in Nairobi? Surely, surely, he would not deliberately lie to a minister of God. Surely not!

But apparently he had fled. His gun bearer was missing, and Jock Davis was dead. Suddenly, Sarah felt she could see nothing good about Peter Stewart. Hadn't he proposed to her and then turned around and proposed to Ruby Davis without even missing a beat? Maybe he wanted to make amends for his terrible guilt. And was all that drinking he had been doing because he was trying to drown his guilt? Sarah's mind reeled.

She heard Anita telling her it was late, and besides, she

was cold. She felt Anita take her arm and lead her inside and down the passageway to her bedroom. She tried to put on a mask that showed concern for Peter's plight, but did not reveal the genuine confusion that she really felt. After all, as far as anyone but Ethel MacDougal knew, Peter was a mere acquaintance in whom she took an interest because she had saved his life.

Sarah knocked briefly on the door to her room and entered quietly. The ladies were already in bed reading. "Good night, Anita!" she announced clearly, so they knew she had not been out walking with a young man. She was glad they turned in early. She hurried with her own preparations for bed, and in minutes she was turning out her light.

She lay there in the darkness, tossing and turning. Peter's guilt suddenly seemed so certain in her churning mind. Then, an hour later, everything had turned over again, and she felt she would stake her life on his innocence. After all, she had brought him back from the brink of death. She knew him. But even as she declared his innocence in her mind, the doubts were already seeping like a slow leak into her thoughts again. For another an hour or so, she was utterly convinced Ruby must be right. Peter Stewart was nothing but a cad!

Her mind seesawed this way until she heard the early dawn birds burst into a blaze of singing and praise for the day that as yet was only a pearly glow in the eastern sky. "This is the day which the Lord hath made; we will rejoice and be glad in it!" she repeated to herself over and over again, trying to block out all her raging emotions. It must have worked because as the sun was flooding the window with a soft pink glow, she dozed off.

eleven

Reg was waiting for Sarah at the entrance to the dining room when she arrived for breakfast, very tired but relieved that the night was over at last. The clear unrelenting light of the day had erased all the shadows in Sarah's mind, and she was disgusted with herself for letting her thoughts and emotions carry her so far from reality during the night. Here in the hard morning light, with Reg smiling at her and steering her to breakfast, she could see clearly that Peter Stewart's business was nothing at all to her. She had done her duty by him. She had helped him recover and told him of the good news of the gospel. Now she must simply shake the dust off her sandals and get on with living her own life.

Her own life was rapidly becoming more interesting. Grace had been said and the porridge was being served, hot and steaming from the kitchen, when Reg leaned over and asked if he might have a few minutes of her time today.

"Of course!" she replied cheerfully, determined to enjoy herself and have as many pleasant conversations with friends as she could squeeze into her week. After the long, dark hours of the night, the day and the solid normalcy of life was such a pleasure to experience. She smiled warmly at Reg. Even he looked happy and wholesome this morning.

"Perhaps after the morning meeting, we might take a

turn in the gardens. We will have about an hour before lunch is served," he said to her, looking nervous and flushed. Sarah was happy to agree with him that a turn in the gardens this morning after the long first meeting would be lovely.

If Sarah had given any thought to the walk in the gardens that morning, she would have been able to guess what was coming, but she didn't. She was tired enough that just concentrating on the speaker, as well as doggedly not thinking about Peter Stewart, took up all her energy. In fact, she had completely forgotten about the walk she had promised Reg, when he hurried up to her as soon as they were dismissed and offered her his arm. She stared at him blankly for a split second before she realized what he meant. She accepted his offer, and he affectionately patted her hand as it rested on his elbow.

It was then that she suddenly realized the reason for Reg's request. Instantly, her heart sank to the bottom of her shoes. She had an overwhelming urge to panic and rush back up to her bedroom, but Reg was leading her briskly outside. She blinked in the bright midday sunshine, and she felt utterly overwhelmed with exhaustion. Reg's voice was rolling above her head, something about what the speaker was telling them this morning and how much he appreciated it.

Sarah let Reg steer her to the very bottom of the garden. A small stream ran along behind a screen of jacaranda trees and flowering shrubs. Reg had obviously been here before, because he led Sarah straight to a little dirt path between the trees and then along the river for a few yards until they came to a mossy log lying along the bank of the stream. "Shall we rest for a moment on this log?" he asked nervously.

Sarah nodded. Her heart was pounding wildly. She knew in her heart of hearts that she wasn't really in love with Reg, at least not yet. But suddenly the thrill of being proposed to, here in this green, lit clearing in a forest, touched her imagination. The romance of it all was so beautiful. Besides, what could be wrong with accepting the proposal of a good Christian man? God would provide her with the appropriate feelings in His own time, if this was meant to be. And underneath it all, she was simply too tired to object to anything He was doing. It actually felt good to succumb to Reg's wishes and just do what he wanted.

She sat on the log, and Reg suddenly dropped right onto his knees before her. She couldn't help noticing that he had accidentally placed one knee in a damp, muddy spot. *He ought to have been more careful,* she thought and wished she could think more romantic thoughts at a time like this. But Reg was taking her hand in his. Sarah braced herself for what was coming. In the back of her mind was the nagging suspicion that she really ought to be enjoying this moment and that there must be something terribly wrong with her because she wasn't.

"My dear Sarah," he began and then cleared his throat nervously and began again. "My dear Sarah, I know we have not known each other a very long time, but I feel I have known you all my life. I suppose it is due to the quick pace of life out here in the colonies where the proper social decorum need not be so strictly adhered to. Although what I am about to say is rather sudden and may come as a surprise to you, I hope you will consider it carefully and prayerfully and give me an answer as soon as you find it in your heart."

"Of course I will, Reg," Sarah managed to say, wondering if other women who were proposed to so romantically ever felt slightly embarrassed about the whole thing too. She decided they didn't and that it was probably some defect in her own makeup and she should ignore the feeling until it went away.

"Sarah," Reg began. "My dear Sarah, would you do me the great honor of becoming my wife? I have fallen in love with you over these past weeks, and you would make me the happiest man in the Empire if you would marry me."

Sarah looked down at his face. Hearing the words come out of the mouth of a real, flesh-and-blood man actually did take her breath away. At last, this was an appropriate sentiment. She never imagined that she would be married at all, let alone be proposed to in such a romantic way, even if it was only Reg. Peter never behaved this way. Again, she swept away that last thought. But the thought of Peter served its purpose. Sarah made up her mind.

"Yes, Reg, I will marry you," she said firmly.

She was gratified by the delight, mixed with intense relief, that spread slowly over Reg's face. "Do you mean it, Sarah? Do you really mean it? You will marry me?"

Sarah laughed. She was in control. It wasn't the romantic dream she had always assumed a marriage proposal ought to be, but real life often didn't live up to the ideals that the romantics of the world tried to say it should. "Yes, Reg, that's what I said. I'll marry you."

He leapt to his feet, slipped on the muddy patch, caught himself, and landed heavily on the log beside Sarah.

She bit her lip so as not to laugh at him.

"Sarah, may I kiss you?"

She turned to face him, but before she knew where he was she had been pecked on the cheek! She shook her head, thinking of Peter's kiss.

"I'm sorry, Sarah. I hope I didn't offend you by kissing you so soon! You have made me the happiest man in Kenya, in Africa, no, in the whole world! Please don't be offended, my dear." Reg was distraught.

Sarah bit her lip again. Perhaps she was just very tired, but this whole experience was making her want to giggle uncontrollably. She turned away from Reg in case he saw her true feelings. She hoped she hadn't made a mistake. But God would surely provide the proper feelings for each other in time. *Oh, Lord, please don't let this be a ghastly mistake. Please make me feel true love, the way it is supposed to be for the man I am to marry.*

Reg took her arm, and they made their way along the river and across the bottom of the garden until the lunch gong was chimed. He was talking all the way, explaining how he had fallen in love with her from the moment that Anita had begun to tell him about her. "It was love before first sight!" He laughed at his own wit, and Sarah, who had been filled with uncontrollable laughter only moments before, couldn't find the humor in this remark.

By the time they had returned to the house, Reg detailed all his feelings about Sarah in the weeks that followed, including the day he had spent at her clinic. He knew that they would make a terrific team, she a nurse and he a doctor. Surely God had brought them together at this time for that very purpose! Anita agreed with him. He didn't know what he would have done if he had not had Anita to unburden himself to these last couple of weeks. She had been a solid rock of understanding and sympathy for him as he went through the difficult struggles he had had with himself as to whether it would be better to remain single, as Saint Paul recommended, or get married so as not to burn with passion. He decided he was burning with passion. Anita agreed.

Sarah made a mental note to ask Anita a little more about Reginald Bingley, since he appeared to have confided his feelings to her rather a lot in the last few weeks.

"Would you mind terribly if I announced our upcoming engagement during lunch, Sarah, my dear? I don't think I can contain my excitement and happiness, but if you object, I will manfully do my best to contain myself."

Sarah cringed inside. Why did she not seem to feel the same level of excitement as he did? She decided again that her feelings were not quite right but that she would pretend they were, until they came into line with what she wanted to do. And what she did want to do was to marry Reginald Bingley. As he had already explained—several times—it was a match made in heaven. Besides, there was no going back, so she may as well let everyone know at once. "Yes, certainly, Reg. I am excited too."

She felt like a hypocrite. Did other women feel this apprehensive about becoming engaged? She had heard stories of women being terrified on their wedding day. Perhaps she was just experiencing that a little early.

When Reg stood up and stammered out his announcement, fairly bursting with pride, Anita gave a squeal of joy and rushed over, the first to hug Sarah. "I knew it!" she whispered in her ear. "He told me he would pop the question today! I'm so glad for him that you said yes!

You have no idea how nervous the poor man was!"

Anita was swept away as a deluge of other people flocked over to hug and kiss Sarah.

The announcement of Reg and Sarah's engagement sent a wave of excitement sweeping over the whole conference. Even Sarah's austere roommates were impressed with her choice of a husband.

"I thoroughly approve of Dr. Reginald Bingley," Miss MacRae informed her as they got ready to go to bed that evening. "He is a polite, earnest young man who has obviously been properly brought up and is sincere about his work in the mission field. There are precious few like him today!"

"Or any day for that matter!" Miss Harrison added excitedly. She was actually giggling girlishly, Sarah noticed in surprise. "If there had been, we might have even been persuaded to marry!"

Sarah found herself laughing along with Miss Harrison and Miss MacRae. Perhaps they were right. After all, she had never seriously considered marriage until Reg Bingley came into the picture. That night, exhausted from lack of sleep and relaxed from laughing, she fell into a deep sleep.

It took her some moments to remember what had happened to her when she awoke the next morning. She had the unformed thought in her mind that something momentous had happened, and Peter's face appeared in her memory for an instant, before suddenly the truth came flooding into her consciousness. Her stomach and her heart dropped. She lay stunned and shocked at these unbidden feelings.

When, oh, when will you make me happy about marrying Reg, Lord? she prayed silently as she sat up and put on her slippers. "It cannot be wrong to be engaged to a Christian man who loves me the way Reg does, can it?"

There was no answer, but the remnants of a hollow feeling echoed around inside her heart while she washed her face and dressed for breakfast.

The excitement was still in the air from their engagement announcement yesterday as Sarah arrived for breakfast. Reg, of course, was waiting anxiously for her by the door and bustled her proudly into the room as the hum of voices stopped for a moment to acknowledge their presence. And it was like that for the rest of the day. Reg stuck to her like glue.

After lunch, she felt almost claustrophobic and explained to him that she needed to lie down for an hour because all the excitement was very tiring. His face fell, but Anita walked past them at that moment. He pecked Sarah quickly on the cheek and rushed after Anita to tell her something important. Sarah went to her room, relieved to be alone even for a few moments.

twelve

As the week wore on, Sarah became more and more tired and found many reasons to go to her room. She was grateful for Anita, who really seemed to enjoy entertaining Reg while Sarah rested. Often when Sarah came downstairs, she walked into the lounge to find the two of them laughing about some joke or new gossip that they had discovered. Reg always jumped up and rushed happily to Sarah's side, where he stuck until she went back to her room. And then Anita was always somewhere nearby.

Sarah was beginning to seriously despair of ever manufacturing the correct feelings for Reg. She had spent many hours on her knees praying. She had argued with God about how perfect a husband Reg would be for her and what a good wife she could be for him, but she needed to feel happier and more excited about the whole thing. The more days that passed, the more worried Sarah became about her lack of feelings. She thought of mentioning her dilemma to Anita, but whenever she was not with Reg, he was with Anita. She wished Ethel had come to the conference. She needed her friendship now, perhaps more than she had ever needed it during the whole time she had known her. Sarah resolved to visit her on the way home. Ethel was a married woman, and she would know what the proper feelings for one's husband were.

At last Saturday evening arrived. The only event left to

attend was the worship service in the morning. Sarah planned to leave as soon as possible because she wanted to stop at the MacDougals' on the way home to tell Ethel about her new situation. She had taken Ralph aside and explained this to him. He agreed. He was on a committee that was meeting for the last time just after the service, so he would arrive home later, anyway. Ethel would be glad for the company, he told her, and she would be thrilled to hear her news. Sarah smiled wanly.

Reg, of course, was not far away, and when she turned to leave the lounge, he was instantly at her side. "I don't know how I am going to manage without seeing you each day!" he whispered dramatically in her ear. "Perhaps we could take a turn in the garden before you go up to bed?"

No! Sarah wanted to protest. But she smiled instead. She must start to feel more excited about marrying Reg, and perhaps one more turn in the garden would do the trick. "That's a lovely idea," she forced herself to say.

Reg puffed up and led her to the door. He reached out to open it for her when someone burst through from the other side and nearly knocked him over.

"Peter!" Sarah didn't know if she said his name aloud or not. But the instant he saw her, he froze. Every cell in her body was clamoring to rush up to him and throw her arms around his neck. But she stood stock-still, her arm through Reg's. She quickly remembered when she had stayed up all night thinking about him. But those thoughts were obviously not far beneath her consciousness because she was instantly awash with the conflicting stories. What was he doing here? she wanted to shout, but she just stood there. So did he.

"I don't believe I know you," Reg said, from far away.

Peter turned to him. "My name is Peter Stewart," he said simply.

"And I am Dr. Reginald Bingley," Reg announced in his most pompous tone. "This is my fiancée, Sarah Cameron. What, may I ask, is your business here at this time of night?"

"Sarah?" said Peter.

"Excuse me, sir, but I asked you to state your business."

"Oh, yes, I came to find Sarah. Sarah Cameron. May I have a word with you in private, Sarah?"

"Sarah Cameron is now my fiancée, Mr., er, Stewart, was it? She does not entertain men alone, especially late at night. Whatever you have to say to her will have to be said in front of me too."

Sarah stared at Reg, not comprehending. She took her arm out of his. "But, Reg, I know Pet—"

"Sarah! You are now my fiancée! I will not have you cavorting alone with strange men who burst through doors unannounced on Saturday nights!"

"That's all right, Sarah, he can come too. I must speak to you, that's all. I am leaving, and I need to speak to you before I go."

The three of them turned to go into the lounge, but there were several knots of people chatting there. They tried the dining room, but the servants were setting up the tables for breakfast already. "Let's go onto the veranda," suggested Sarah, feeling suddenly that if she didn't breathe some fresh air, she might faint. She couldn't conceive of Reg and Peter being in the same place, breathing the same air, even. They belonged to different worlds, they lived on different planes, they should never interact. Especially not here and not now.

Reg marched through the door and held it open for Sarah. Peter followed her. Sarah suddenly felt like a prisoner in Reg's world. She was now tied to his world, and she would never be able to skip off into Peter's again. She gulped the night air. Reg stood before her, his arms crossed, stern and cold. He was obviously exercising his new authority over her to the fullest. The begging suitor, the excitable groom, had vanished. He had now become lord and master of her. Even before they had spoken their vows, before she had promised to love, cherish, and obey him, he expected that she obey him. Had she really given this man such power over her already?

Peter came to her side. "Sarah, I didn't realize you were engaged. May I offer my congratulations?"

It was the flattest, most empty congratulations she had received all week. She realized with a brief burst of pleasure that Peter was not happy that she was engaged. He shook her hand. The touch of his fingers on her bare skin burned right through her body so quickly it took away her breath. He shook Reg's hand. Reg softened for an instant and smiled. There was an awkward silence for a moment. Peter glanced at Reg quickly before turning back to Sarah. She felt as though they were being watched by a guard in a prison. But Peter was looking right into her eyes, as if he were trying to pretend that there were only the two of them out on the veranda.

"Sarah," he said, her name a nervous quaver. "I came to tell you that I have made a very important decision, and it is one that I think you have much to do with." He glanced over at Reg again. Reg was standing with his feet apart and his arms crossed over his chest.

"I want to thank you for all your prayers for me. They

have not gone unanswered. I decided last week when I was staying at the French mission to accept Jesus Christ as my Lord and Savior."

"Oh, Peter! I am so glad, so very glad." She wanted to fling her arms around him and hug him, but she could literally feel Reg's eyes boring into her, and she was afraid. She stood staring at Peter for a long moment, and suddenly the thought came to her that if she couldn't hug someone who had just changed the course of his entire life, and the life to come, perhaps she had a heart of stone. She did not! She flung her arms around him and hugged him.

"Excuse me, Sarah, I would like to shake the man's hand." A cold, hard voice seemed to cut between them like a knife. Sarah let Peter go as if he were a hot coal. Reg stepped forward and shook Peter's hand again. "Congratulations on making a momentous decision, Mr. Stewart. I have heard of your exploits in the past, and I know you have not lived a morally upright life. But Jesus Christ is capable of forgiving even the most heinous sins, if you simply confess them to. . ."

Sarah was appalled. What was Reg talking about? He seemed to be implying that Peter was a depraved sinner, certainly more depraved than an ordinary new Christian. Did he know about Ruby's accusations? If he did, he obviously believed them wholeheartedly. Who had told him?

And before she had even asked herself the question, she knew the answer. Anita, of course! All those afternoons he had spent with Anita, they must have been talking about something. She had flattered herself that all Reg and Anita discussed would be the engagement. But now it was obvious that Anita had told him all about

Peter and Ruby and how Ruby was claiming that it was Peter's fault that Jock had been killed by the rhino.

Peter was staring at Reg, openmouthed, but his eyes were burning. Sarah could tell that he was trying to hide his fury. Reg was discussing how Jesus had forgiven the murderer who was crucified next to Him.

"Reg! Stop! Peter is a brand-new Christian. You have no call to be lecturing him on murderers!"

"I think perhaps I have, Sarah. I have certain information that you clearly know nothing about. And besides, Mr. Stewart has given you his news now. You are obviously very glad to receive it, but there is more to being a Christian than saying you are committed to Jesus and then going around begging for hugs from overly emotional women! And the sooner he learns about the more serious side of his faith, the better."

"Dr. Bingley, I am perfectly aware of the serious side of the Christian faith, and I am also aware of the information you claim to possess about me, information which I might add is—"

Reg interrupted by turning to Sarah. "Sarah, I believe that Mr. Stewart is about to discuss matters that are rather indelicate. As my fiancée, you should not be exposed to such information. Wait for me in the parlor. Anita will be happy to keep you company until Mr. Stewart and I are finished."

"Excuse me, Dr. Bingley." Sarah did not even try to mitigate the sarcasm freezing in her voice. "But I have certain unpleasant information about Mr. Stewart that you do not possess. For example, it was I who saved his life after he was trampled and gored by a rhinoceros. I feel I can listen to such issues without resorting to smelling salts and shrieks of horror. I intend to stay."

"And I say, go. You will listen to me. I am about to become your husband, and I will not have you disobeying me. You will go inside at once, or you will forfeit your claim to our future marriage." Reg's lip curled to an ugly snarl as he spoke, or rather hissed, the last sentence at her.

Sarah was so angry she could hardly stammer her response. "I do not forfeit my marriage! I throw it in your face!" She turned, forgetting Peter, and stormed down the veranda steps.

"Fine. I wash my hands of you!"

Reg's voice struck out into the empty air behind her, and she heard the slam of the door. He had gone inside. She smiled grimly as she charged out of the gate and down the road. She had no idea where she was going. She could hardly even see as tears of fury suddenly came streaming down her cheeks. How could she have been so incredibly stupid as to engage herself to Reginald Bingley?

Footsteps came pattering along the hard, dirt road behind her. She was only dimly aware of them. Someone took her arm. She let out a shriek and turned. It was Peter. For the first time in months she had actually forgotten about him! But at the sight of his face, so familiar, and so filled with care and concern for her, she burst into tears. He took her in his arms, and they stood for a long time until she had cried all the anger and rage out of her system. Then silently, mutually, they turned and walked into the night of the newborn city.

Lights from windows flickered dimly behind drawn curtains as they passed along the road in front of verandas and gardens. They could smell the smoke of the African night fires wafting in the distance through the darkness. Peter walked with his arm around Sarah's shoulder as though they were old, old friends. Perhaps they were. Their friendship had seen more turmoil in these few months than most friendships in a whole lifetime.

After they had walked a little while, Peter began to talk. "I'm glad that you turned down my proposal, Sarah," he said. "I don't know what I was thinking."

Sarah stopped walking and stared at him. Surely he wasn't taking Reg's side and telling her that she would make a disobedient, bad wife.

But when he saw the look on her face, he laughed and took her hand. "No, Sarah, I don't mean it that way. I just mean that by turning me down you made me take a good look at myself. I can't blame Dr. Bingley for what he said about me to you tonight, because when I wanted to marry you, I was probably even more arrogant than he is. And you put me in my place, just as you put him in his place tonight. Perhaps after awhile you will find it in your heart to forgive him, and you will marry him after all."

Sarah was silent. He didn't know that breaking off her engagement to Reg was more of a relief than a tragedy. She realized that she felt lighter and freer than she had in the whole week she had been engaged. She was no longer expected to be in Reg's company everyday. She did not need to hide her true feelings and try to manufacture happiness anymore. It was such a tremendous relief.

Without thinking she stepped away from Peter's side and pirouetted around and around like a little girl, letting her skirt fly out around her ankles and staring up at the stars spinning in the sky above her.

"Sarah! What are you doing? I've been so selfish! I'll just take you right back to the Mission House so you can make up with Reg. I should have done that at once. I'm sorry."

Sarah stopped pirouetting. "I don't want to make up with Reg. I'm just so happy to be free!" She spun around a couple more times, and suddenly she felt Peter catch her by the waist, and he waltzed her down the street spinning around and around until they were both laughing so hard, tears were flowing down Sarah's cheeks.

They got dizzy and stopped. Sarah clutched Peter's arm to steady herself, and they walked on in silence. Sarah reveled in the silence. How could she have convinced herself that she would be able to put up with Reg Bingley's constant chatter for the rest of her life? What could she have been thinking? It was such a tremendous relief not to be engaged to him anymore. She glanced at Peter, walking along beside her. He seemed to be lost in thought. How funny that when she turned down Peter's proposal, relief was the last thing she felt.

Peter began to talk in a quiet, pensive voice, as if he were speaking to himself. "I know what Reg was referring to when he said that he had information about me. It's all over Nairobi and probably the whole colony by now too. Of course Ruby was angry when I broke off our engagement. She had every right to be. I don't blame her at all. I should never have asked her to marry me. I wasn't really in love with her. I was just trying to pretend to myself and to her that I was. It was entirely unfair to her. And Ruby has never been the type of person to take humiliation lying down. I think she truly believes in her heart that it was my fault that Jock was killed by the rhino."

Sarah couldn't bear to hear Peter blaming himself for Ruby's lies. "But, Peter," she burst out, "it was not your fault!"

"It's my safari, Sarah. He died on my watch. Whether or not it was my fault, his life was my responsibility."

"But even so, that's no reason to let Ruby spread all these ugly rumors about you. You couldn't stop Juma from firing his gun. And you did everything you could to save Jock. You nearly gave your own life in the attempt. Why doesn't anyone believe that? You can't let Ruby do this to your reputation, Peter; you simply cannot!"

Peter looked down at her face, blazing with passion and anger. A slow mysterious smile spread across his own face, and then it was gone. He turned away, and they walked on into the dark night. Lights were beginning to be extinguished in the houses they passed. It was getting very late.

"What will happen to your safari business, Peter, if you don't put a stop to Ruby's false accusations? Not to mention your own personal reputation!"

"Dr. Bingley was absolutely right when he reminded me that I am a sinner. Only I don't need to be reminded. I accept it, I have confessed it, and I pray that by the grace of God, I am forgiven for my sins. But the consequences of my sin still exist, and I must deal with them. People no longer want to go on safari with me. I don't blame them, even if they don't know the whole story. And I don't care about my personal reputation anymore. I am hidden in Christ. That's all that matters to me. So, I will not fight against Ruby's attacks on my reputation. I have done her enough harm already."

"Then what will you do, Peter?" Sarah asked desperately. "Your whole life is ruined. Did I save your life so that Ruby could ruin it like this?"

They were on the outskirts of town now. Farmers' fields lined each side of the road, which had become a rougher track. Sarah had stumbled a couple of times in the dark night. Peter took her arm again. He steered her to a wooden fence that ran alongside the road. They climbed up on the rails and sat, looking out over the African sky. It was breathtakingly beautiful. Sarah didn't think she had ever seen the sky looking more rich and velvet than it did tonight. And the stars twinkled more brightly, and there were so many of them, they outnumbered the grains of sand below.

Peter spoke now, in answer to her question. "That's why I came to talk to you tonight, Sarah. I wanted you to know that I am going back to Aberdeen next week."

"Next week! You mean you are just going to give up and go back to Scotland with your tail between your legs? Just because of a woman like Ruby Davis? Peter, you can't give up so easily!" Sarah stopped suddenly, embarrassed at the passion in her own voice. She had no right to tell Peter that he couldn't go back to Scotland.

"No, not with my tail between my legs. And not because of Ruby Davis. Because of you, Sarah."

"What? But I don't want you to go, Peter. Please don't go!"

"Wait and let me finish what I am trying to tell you, Sarah. I am going back to Aberdeen to go to medical school. My father has been telling me to be a doctor all my life. I was rebelling against him, and that's why I came out here in the first place. God has taken the terrible situation between me and Ruby and turned it into a good thing for me. He's made me realize that I should go back home, like the prodigal son. I must ask my father to forgive me and go to medical school as I should have done many years ago. And if it weren't for your prayers and work that saved my life, and if you had not turned down my proposal, I would never have come to the end of my rope. I would never have seen that God is my salvation. I would still be running away from my responsibilities. I am grateful for everything that has happened, Sarah." He paused, took a deep breath, and turned to face her. "And I am grateful for you, Sarah."

"Will you ever come back, Peter?" Sarah's voice was small, almost lost in the vast black night.

"Yes, nothing could keep me from coming back."

"I'll miss you."

"I will think of you every single day, Sarah."

"I'll think of you too, Peter."

Peter got off the fence. He stood in front of Sarah and took a deep breath. Sarah felt a warm rush of joy burst over her. There was no mistaking her feelings this time. She looked down into his familiar blue eyes, and her heart started to beat quickly. This must be love.

"Will you wait for me, Sarah?"

"With all my heart, Peter."

He reached out and took her into his arms.

Much later, Peter and Sarah walked back to the Mission House. They were tired from walking and talking late into the night. One light was on in the house. Sarah and Peter walked quietly up the steps of the veranda. The light was in the lounge. Two people were talking together in low voices, and Sarah glanced through the open window. It was Reg and Anita. They were sitting together on the couch, deep in conversation. Sarah looked up at Peter. They didn't say anything, but they both knew that Reg would get over the loss of Sarah very well.

Peter kissed Sarah one last time and whispered, "Will you come to church with me in the morning? I'll drive over and fetch you." Sarah nodded and silently opened the front door. She would begin her new life worshipping God with Peter Stewart. He had truly come home at last.

A Letter To Our Readers

Dear Reader:

In order that we might better contribute to your reading enjoyment, we would appreciate your taking a few minutes to respond to the following questions. We welcome your comments and read each form and letter we receive. When completed, please return to the following:

Rebecca Germany, Fiction Editor
Heartsong Presents
PO Box 719
Uhrichsville, Ohio 44683

1. Did you enjoy reading *With Healing in His Wings* by Sally Krueger?
   ❑ Very much! I would like to see more books by this author!
   ❑ Moderately. I would have enjoyed it more if

_____

_____

2. Are you a member of **Heartsong Presents**? Yes ❑ No ❑
   If no, where did you purchase this book?_____

   _____

3. How would you rate, on a scale from 1 (poor) to 5 (superior), the cover design?_____

4. On a scale from 1 (poor) to 10 (superior), please rate the following elements.

   _____ Heroine   _____ Plot

   _____ Hero   _____ Inspirational theme

   _____ Setting   _____ Secondary characters

5. These characters were special because_____

_____

_____

6. How has this book inspired your life?_____

_____

_____

7. What settings would you like to see covered in future
   Heartsong Presents books?_____

_____

_____

8. What are some inspirational themes you would like to see
   treated in future books?_____

_____

_____

9. Would you be interested in reading other **Heartsong
   Presents** titles?   Yes ❏   No ❏

10. Please check your age range:
    ❏ Under 18   ❏ 18-24   ❏ 25-34
    ❏ 35-45   ❏ 46-55   ❏ Over 55

Name _____

Occupation _____

Address _____

City _____ State _____ Zip _____

Email _____

Woven Hearts

The Steadman Mill is the heart of industry in Eastead, Massachusetts. The Kindred Hearts Orphanage is the pulse of the town's charity efforts. . .and, most recently, the focus of a wave of change.

The Steadman Mill has begun to offer work to Kindred Hearts girls. Now the young women are stepping into leadership positions within the mill and the community—and stealing the hearts of the town's most eligible bachelors in the process.

Take a journey with four women of Eaststead as they balance their gentle natures with newly discovered strength of character. They have placed their souls in God's hands. . .now, will they trust Him with their hearts, too?

paperback, 352 pages, 5 ³⁄₁₆" x 8"

♥ ♥ ♥ ♥ ♥ ♥ ♥ ♥ ♥ ♥ ♥ ♥ ♥ ♥ ♥ ♥ ♥ ♥

Please send me _____ copies of *Woven Hearts*. I am enclosing $6.97 for each. (Please add $2.00 to cover postage and handling per order. OH add 6% tax.)

Send check or money order, no cash or C.O.D.s please.

Name_____

Address _____

City, State, Zip _____

To place a credit card order, call 1-800-847-8270.

Send to: Heartsong Presents Reader Service, PO Box 721, Uhrichsville, OH 44683

♥ ♥ ♥ ♥ ♥ ♥ ♥ ♥ ♥ ♥ ♥ ♥ ♥ ♥ ♥ ♥ ♥ ♥

Hearts♥ng Presents
Love Stories Are Rated G!

That's for godly, gratifying, and of course, great! If you love a thrilling love story but don't appreciate the sordidness of some popular paperback romances, **Heartsong Presents** is for you. In fact, **Heartsong Presents** is the *only inspirational romance book club* featuring love stories where Christian faith is the primary ingredient in a marriage relationship.

Sign up today to receive your first set of four never-before-published Christian romances. Send no money now; you will receive a bill with the first shipment. You may cancel at any time without obligation, and if you aren't completely satisfied with any selection, you may return the books for an immediate refund!

Imagine...four new romances every four weeks—two historical, two contemporary—with men and women like you who long to meet the one God has chosen as the love of their lives...all for the low price of $10.99 postpaid.

To join, simply complete the coupon below and mail to the address provided. **Heartsong Presents** romances are rated G for another reason: They'll arrive *Godspeed!*